The Diamond Pin

By Carolyn Wells

Originally published in 1919

The Diamond Pin

© 2013 Resurrected Press
www.ResurrectedPress.com

Published by Resurrected Press

This classic book was handcrafted by Resurrected Press. Resurrected Press is dedicated to bringing high quality classic books back to the readers who enjoy them. These are not scanned versions of the originals, but, rather, quality checked and edited books meant to be enjoyed!

Please visit ResurrectedPress.com to view our entire catalogue!

ISBN 13: 978-1-937022-65-5

Printed in the United States of America

RESURRECTED PRESS CLASSIC MYSTERY CATALOGUE

Journeys into Mystery
Travel and Mystery in a More Elegant Time

The Edwardian Detectives
Literary Sleuths of the Edwardian Era

Gems of Mystery
Lost Jewels from a More Elegant Age

Anne Austin
One Drop of Blood
The Black Pigeon
Murder at Bridge

E. C. Bentley
Trent's Last Case: The Woman in Black

Ernest Bramah
Max Carrados Resurrected:
The Detective Stories of Max Carrados

Agatha Christie
The Secret Adversary
The Mysterious Affair at Styles

Octavus Roy Cohen
Midnight

Freeman Wills Croft
The Ponson Case
The Pit Prop Syndicate

J. S. Fletcher

Sir William Magnay
The Hunt Ball Mystery

Mabel and Paul Thorne
The Sheridan Road Mystery

Louis Tracy
The Strange Case of Mortimer Fenley
The Albert Gate Mystery
The Bartlett Mystery
The Postmaster's Daughter
The House of Peril
The Sandling Case: What Would You Have Done?

Charles Edmonds Walk
The Paternoster Ruby

John R. Watson
The Mystery of the Downs
The Hampstead Mystery

Edgar Wallace
The Daffodil Mystery
The Crimson Circle

Carolyn Wells
Vicky Van
The Man Who Fell Through the Earth
In the Onyx Lobby
Raspberry Jam
The Clue
The Room with the Tassels
The Vanishing of Betty Varian
The Mystery Girl
The White Alley
The Curved Blades
Anybody but Anne

The Bride of a Moment
Faulkner's Folly
The Diamond Pin
The Gold Bag
The Mystery of the Sycamore
The Come Back

Raoul Whitfield
Death in a Bowl

And much more!
Visit ResurrectedPress.com
for our complete catalogue

FOREWORD

Before she turned to writing mysteries, Carolyn Wells was known for writing humorous verse and books of puzzles and riddles. It is no surprise then, that practical jokes should feature in one of her many mysteries, and from the first ink filled fig this would seem to be the case. But when the jokester is discovered dead, *The Diamond Pin* takes a more serious turn.

As with most of her mysteries, Wells is as interested in the social aspects of the crime as the actual business of their commission and detection. In this case, it is the stress of the missing legacy and the reactions of the various characters to the plight of the nephew when all the clues seem to implicate him as the murderer. It should be said that the main characters are shown in a better light than in many of Wells' books, with the possible exception of the victim, who does come off as something of a tiresome eccentric.

Still, there are plenty of the usual trappings of mysteries of the time to hold the reader's attention. There is, of course, the locked room and its corpse. But there is also the secret of the location of the hoard of gems hidden by the victim and forming the legacy of her niece and nephew. And in the grand tradition of vintage mysteries, there is the puzzle of the pin which may, or may not, lead to the recovery of the jewels, and even at the end, a cryptogram to be solved.

Early in her career of writing mysteries, Carolyn Wells was thought by many to be a bit over fond of secret panels, hidden passages, and other "architectural devices" as a solution to her crimes, but in *The Diamond Pin* she chooses a completely different means to release herself from the dilemma of the locked room, demonstrating that she was not a one dimensional writer.

Unusual, too, is the amount of action taking place. While most of her mysteries are primarily cerebral in nature, with questions posed and answered, in *The Diamond Pin*, Iris Clyde, the niece seems to be facing midnight intruders armed with pistols and kidnappers at every turn as some unseen villain tries to deprive her of the pin which holds the clue to the puzzle of the hidden gems. And Fleming Stone, one of Wells' favorite detectives, makes his appearance a number of chapters earlier than is his usual practice taking a more active role than usual.

The Diamond Pin has many of the feature that made Carolyn Wells such a popular writer of mysteries in the early part of the twentieth century. It is with great pleasure that Resurrected Press presents this new edition for your enjoyment.

About the Author

Carolyn Wells, June 18, 1862 March 26, 1942 was an American writer and poet. She was best known for her books of poetry and humor until around 1910 she read one of Anna Katherine Green's mysteries and took up the genre. Many of her mysteries featured the detective Fleming Stone. She was married to Hadwin Houghton, heir to the Houghton-Mifflin publishing company. She was a collector of poetry by other authors, and, upon her death, she bequeathed her collection of the works of Walt Witman to the Library of Congress.

Greg Fowlkes
Editor-In-Chief
Resurrected Press
www.ResurrectedPress.com

TABLE OF CONTENTS

CHAPTER 1: A CERTAIN DATE

"Well, go to church then, and I hope to goodness you'll come back in a more spiritual frame of mind! Though how you can feel spiritual in that flibbertigibbet dress is more than I know! An actress, indeed! No mummers' masks have ever blotted the scutcheon of my family tree. The Clydes were decent, God-fearing people, and I don't propose, Miss, that you shall disgrace the name."

Ursula Pell shook her good-looking gray head and glowered at her pretty niece, who was getting into a comfortable though not elaborate motor car.

"I know you didn't propose it, Aunt Ursula," returned the smiling girl, "I thought up the scheme myself, and I decline to let you have credit of its origin."

"Discredit, you mean," and Mrs. Pell sniffed haughtily. "Here's some money for the contribution plate. Iris; see that you put it in, and don't appropriate it yourself."

The slender, aristocratic old hand, half covered by a falling lace frill, dropped a coin into Iris' out-held palm, and the girl perceived it was one cent.

She looked at her aunt in amazement, for Mrs. Pell was a millionaire; then, thinking better of her impulse to voice an indignant protest, Iris got into the car. Immediately, she saw a dollar bill on the seat beside her and she knew that was for the contribution plate, and the penny was a joke of her aunt's.

For Ursula Pell had a queer twist in her fertile old brain that made her enjoy the temporary discomfiture of her friends, whenever she was able to bring it about. To see anyone chagrined, nonplused, or made suddenly to feel ridiculous, was to Mrs. Pell an occasion of sheer delight.

To do her justice, her whimsical tricks usually ended in the gratification of the victim in some way, as now, when Iris, thinking her aunt had given her a penny for the collection, found the dollar ready for that worthy cause. But such things are irritating, and were particularly so to Iris Clyde, whose sense of humor was of a different trend.

In fact, Iris' whole nature was different from her aunt's, and therein lay most of the difficulties of their living together. For there were difficulties. The erratic, emphatic, dogmatic old lady could not sympathize with the high-strung, high-spirited young girl, and as a result there was more friction than should be in any well-regulated family.

And Mrs. Pell had a decided penchant for practical jokes—than which there is nothing more abominable. But members of Mrs. Pell's household put up with these because if they didn't they automatically ceased to be members of Mrs. Pell's household.

One member had made this change. A nephew, Winston Bannard, had resented his aunt's gift of a trick cigar, which blew up and sent fine sawdust into his eyes and nose, and her follow-up of a box of Perfectos was insufficient to keep him longer in the uncertain atmosphere of her otherwise pleasant country home.

And now, Iris Clyde had announced her intention of leaving the old roof also. Her pretext was that she wanted to become an actress, and that was true, but had Mrs Pell been more companionable and easy to live with, Iris would have curbed her histrionic ambitions. Nor is it beyond the possibilities that Iris chose the despised profession, because she knew it would enrage her aunt to think of a Clyde going into the depths of ignominy which the stage represented to Mrs. Pell.

For Iris Clyde at twenty-two had quite as strong a will and inflexible a determination as her aunt at sixty-two, and though they oftenest ran parallel, yet when they criss-crossed, neither was ready to yield the fraction of a point for the sake of peace in the family.

And it was after one of their most heated discussions, after a duel of words that flicked with sarcasm and rasped with innuendo, that Iris, cool and pretty in her summer costume, started for church, leaving Mrs. Pell, irate and still nervously quivering from her own angry tirade.

Iris smiled and waved the bill at her aunt as the car started, and then suddenly looked aghast and leaned over the side of the car as if she had dropped the dollar. But the car sped on, and Iris waved frantically, pointing to the spot where she had seemed to drop the bill, and motioning her aunt to go out there and get it.

This Mrs. Pell promptly did, only to be rewarded by a ringing laugh from Iris and a wave of the bill in the girl's hand, as the car slid through the gates and out of sight.

"Silly thing!" grumbled Ursula Pell, returning to the piazza where she had been sitting. But she smiled at the way her niece had paid her back in her own coin, if a dollar bill can be considered coin.

This, then, was the way the members of the Pell household were expected to conduct themselves. Nor was it only the family, but the servants also were frequent butts for the misplaced hilarity of their mistress.

One cook left because of a tiny mouse imprisoned in her workbasket; one first-class gardener couldn't stand a scarecrow made in a ridiculous caricature of himself; and one small scullery maid objected to unexpected and startling "Boos!" from dark corners.

But servants could always be replaced, and so, for that matter, could relatives, for Mrs. Pell had many kinsfolk, and her wealth would prove a strong magnet to most of them.

Indeed, as outsiders often exclaimed, why mind a harmless joke now and then? Which was all very well—for the outsiders. But it is far from pleasant to live in continual expectation of salt in one's tea or cotton in one's croquettes.

So Winston had picked up his law books and sought refuge in New York City and Iris, after a year's further endurance, was thinking seriously of following suit.

And yet, Ursula Pell was most kind, generous and indulgent. Iris had been with her for ten years, and as a child or a very young girl, she had not minded her aunt's idiosyncrasy, had, indeed, rather enjoyed the foolish tricks. But, of late, they had bored her, and their constant recurrence so wore on her nerves that she wanted to go away and order her life for herself. The stage attracted her, though not insistently. She planned to live in bachelor apartments with a girl chum who was an artist, and hoped to find congenial occupation of some kind. She rather harped on the actress proposition because it so thoroughly annoyed her aunt, and matters between them had now come to such a pass, that they teased each other in any and every way possible. This was entirely Mrs. Pell's fault, for if she hadn't had her peculiar trait of practical joking, Iris never would have dreamed of teasing her.

On the whole, they were good friends, and often a few days would pass in perfect harmony by reason of Ursula not being moved by her imp of the perverse to cut up any silly prank. Then, Iris would drink from a glass of water, to find it had been tinctured with asafetida, or brush her hair and then learn that some drops of glue had been put on the bristles of her hairbrush.

Anger or sulks at these performances were just what Mrs. Pell wanted, so Iris roared with laughter and pretended to think it all very funny, whereupon Mrs. Pell did the sulking, and Iris scored.

So it was not, perhaps, surprising that the girl concluded to leave her aunt's home and shift for herself. It would, she knew, probably mean disinheritance; but after all money is not everything, and as the old lady grew older, her pranks became more and more an intolerable nuisance.

And Iris wanted to go out into the world and meet people. The neighbors in the small town of Berrien, where they lived, were uninteresting, and there were few visitors from the outside world. Though less than fifteen miles from New York, Iris rarely invited her friends to visit her because of the probability that her aunt would play some absurd trick on them. This had happened so many times, even though Mrs. Pell had promised that it should not occur, that Iris had resolved never to try it again.

The best friends and advisers of the girl were Mr. Bowen, the rector, and his wife. The two were also friends of Mrs. Pell, and perhaps out of respect for his cloth, the old lady never played tricks on the Bowens. It was their habit to dine every Sunday at Pellbrook, and the occasion was always the pleasantest of the whole week.

The farm was a large one, about a mile from the village, and included old-fashioned orchards and hayfields as well as more modern greenhouses and gardens. There was a lovely brook, a sunny slope of hillside, and a delightful grove of maples, and added to these a long-distance view of hazy hills that made Pellbrook one of the most attractive country places for many miles around.

Ursula Pell sat on her verandah quite contentedly gazing over the landscape and thinking about her multitudinous affairs.

"I s'pose I oughtn't to tease that child," she thought, smiling at the recollection; "I don't know what I'd do, if she should leave me! Win went, but, land! you can't keep a young man down! A girl, now, 's different. I guess I'll take Iris to New York next winter and let her have a little fling. I'll pretend I'm going alone, and leave her here to keep the house, and then I'll take her too! She'll be so surprised!"

The old lady's eyes twinkled and she fairly reveled in the joke she would play on her niece. And, not to do her an injustice, she meant no harm. She really thought only of the girl's glad surprise at learning she was to go, and gave no heed to the misery that might be caused by the previous disappointment.

A woman came out from the house to ask directions for dinner.

"Yes, Polly," said Ursula Pell, "the Bowens will dine here as usual. Dinner at one-thirty, sharp, as the rector has to leave at three, to attend some meeting or other. Pity they had to have it on Sunday."

There was some discussion of the menu and then Polly, the old cook, shuffled away, and again Ursula Pell sat alone.

"An actress!" she ruminated, "my little Iris an actress! Well, I guess not! But I can persuade her out of that foolishness, I'll bet! Why, if I can't do it any other way, I'll take her traveling,—I'll—why, I'll give her her inheritance now, and let her amuse herself being an heiress before I'm dead and gone. Why should I wait for that, any way? Suppose I give her the pin at once—I'd do it to-day, I believe, while the notion's on me, if I only had it here. I can get it from Mr. Chapin in a few days, and then—well, then, Iris would have something to interest her! I wonder how she'd like a whole king's ransom of jewels! She's like a princess herself. And, then, too, that girl ought to marry, and marry well. I suppose I ought to have been thinking about this before. I must talk to the Bowens—of course, there's no one in Berrien—I did think one time Win might fall in love with her, but then he went away, and now he never comes up here any more. I wonder if Iris cares especially for Win. She never says anything about him, but that's no sign, one way or the other. I'd like her to marry Roger Downing, but she snubs him unmercifully. And he is a little countrified. With Iris' beauty and the fortune I shall leave her, she could marry anybody on earth! I believe I'll take her traveling a bit, say, to California, and then spend the winter in New York and give the girl a chance. And I must quit teasing her. But I do love to see that surprised look when I play some outlandish trick on her!"

The old lady's eyes assumed a vixenish expression and her smile widened till it was a sly, almost diabolical grin. Quite evidently she was even then planning some new and particularly disagreeable joke on Iris.

At length she rose and went into the house to write in her diary. Ursula Pell was of most methodical habits, and a daily journal was regularly kept.

The main part of the house was four square, a wide hall running straight through the center, with doors front and back. On the left, as one entered, the big living room was in front, and behind it a smaller sitting room, which was Mrs. Pell's own. Not that anyone was unwelcome there, but it held many of her treasures and individual belongings, and served as her study or office, for the transaction of the various business matters in which she was involved. Frequently her lawyer was closeted with her here for long confabs, for Ursula Pell was greatly given to the pleasurable entertainment of changing her will.

She had made more wills than Lawyer Chapin could count, and each in turn was duly drawn up and witnessed and the previous one destroyed. Her diary usually served to record the changes she proposed making, and when the time was ripe for a new will, the diary was requisitioned for direction as to the testamentary document.

The wealth of Ursula Pell was enormous, far more so than one would suppose from the simplicity of her household appointments. This was not due to miserliness, but to her simple tastes and her frugal early life. Her fortune was the bequest of her husband, who, now dead more than twenty years, had amassed a great deal of money which he had invested almost entirely in precious stones. It was his theory and belief that stocks and bonds were uncertain, whereas gems were always valuable. His collection included some world-famous diamonds and rubies, and a set of emeralds that were historic.

But nobody, save Ursula Pell herself, knew where these stones were. Whether in safe deposit or hidden on her own property, she had never given so much as a hint to her family or her lawyer. James Chapin knew his eccentric old client better than to inquire concerning the whereabouts of her treasure, and made and remade the wills disposing of it, without comment. A few of the smaller gems Mrs. Pell had given to Iris and to young Bannard, and some, smaller still, to more distant relatives; but the bulk of the collection had never been seen by the present generation.

She often told Iris that it should all be hers eventually, but Iris didn't seriously bank on the promise, for she knew her erratic aunt might quite conceivably will the jewels to some distant cousin, in a moment of pique at her niece.

For Iris was not diplomatic. Never had she catered to her aunt's whims or wishes with a selfish motive. She honestly tried to live peaceably with Mrs. Pell, but of late she had begun to believe that impossible, and was planning to go away.

As usual on Sunday morning, Ursula Pell had her house to herself.

Her modest establishment consisted of only four servants, who engaged additional help as their duties required. Purdy, the old gardener, was the husband of Polly, the cook; Agnes, the waitress, also served as ladies' maid when occasion called for it. Campbell, the chauffeur, completed the menage, and all other workers, and there were a good many, were employed by the day, and did not live at Pellbrook.

Mrs. Pell rarely went to church, and on Sunday mornings Campbell took Iris to the village. Agnes accompanied them, as she, too, attended the Episcopal service.

Purdy and his wife drove an old horse and still older buckboard to a small church nearby, which better suited their type of piety.

Polly was a marvel of efficiency and managed cleverly to go to meeting without in any way delaying or interfering with her preparations for the Sunday dinner. Indeed, Ursula Pell would have no one around her who was not efficient. Waste and waste motion were equally taboo in that household.

The mistress of the place made her customary round of the kitchen quarters, and, finding everything in its usual satisfactory condition, returned to her own sitting room, and took her diary from her desk.

At half-past twelve the Purdys returned, and at one o'clock the motor car brought its load from the village.

"Well, well, Mr. Bowen, how do you do?" the hostess greeted them as they arrived. "And dear Mrs. Bowen, come right in and lay off your bonnet."

The wide hall, with its tables, chairs and mirrors offered ample accommodations for hats and wraps, and soon the party were seated on the front part of the broad verandah that encircled three sides of the house.

Mr. Bowen was stout and jolly and his slim shadow of a wife acted as a sort of Greek chorus, agreeing with and echoing his remarks and opinions.

Conversation was in a gay and bantering key, and Mrs. Pell was in high good humor. Indeed, she seemed nervously excited and a little hysterical, but this was not entirely unusual, and her guests fitted their mood to hers.

A chance remark led to mention of Mrs. Pell's great fortune of jewels, and Mr. Bowen declared that he fully expected she would bequeath them all to his church to be made into a wonderful chalice.

"Not a bad idea," exclaimed Ursula Pell; "and one I've never thought of! I'll get Mr. Chapin over here to-morrow to change my will."

"Who will be the loser?" asked the rector. "To whom are they willed at present?"

"That's telling," and Mrs. Pell smiled mysteriously.

"Don't forget you've promised me the wonderful diamond pin, auntie," said Iris, bristling up a little.

"What diamond pin?" asked Mrs. Bowen, curiously.

"Oh, for years, Aunt Ursula has promised me a marvelous diamond pin, the most valuable of her whole collection—haven't you, auntie?"

"Yes, Iris," and Mrs. Pell nodded her head, "that pin is certainly the most valuable thing I possess."

"It must be a marvel, then," said Mr. Bowen, his eyes opening wide, "for I've heard great tales of the Pell collection. I thought they were all unset jewels."

"Most of them are," Mrs. Pell spoke carelessly, "but the pin I shall leave to Iris——"

At that moment dinner was announced, and the group went to the dining room. This large and pleasant room was in front on the right, and back of it were the pantries and kitchens. A long rear extension provided the servants' quarters, which were numerous and roomy. The house was comfortable rather than pretentious, and though the village folk wondered why so rich a woman continued to live in such an old-fashioned home, those who knew her well realized that the place exactly met Ursula Pell's requirements.

The dinner was in harmony with the atmosphere of the home. Plentiful, well-cooked food there was, but no attempt at elaborate confections or any great formality of service.

One concession to modernity was a small dish of stuffed dates at each cover, and of these Mrs. Pell spoke in scornful tones.

"Some of Iris' foolishness," she observed. "She wants all sorts of knick-knacks that she considers stylish!"

"I don't at all, auntie," denied the girl, flushing with annoyance, "but when you ate those dates at Mrs. Graham's the other day, you enjoyed them so much I thought I'd make some. She gave me her recipe, and I think they're very nice."

"I do, too," agreed Mrs. Bowen, eating a date appreciatively, and feeling sorry for Iris' discomfiture. For though many girls might not mind such disapproval, Iris was of a sensitive nature, and cringed beneath her aunt's sharp words.

In an endeavor to cover her embarrassment, she picked up a date from her own portion and bit off the end.

From the fruit spurted a stream of jet black ink, which stained Iris' lips, offended her palate, and spilling on her pretty white frock, utterly ruined the dainty chiffon and lace.

She comprehended instantly. Her aunt, to annoy her, had managed to conceal ink in one of the dates, and place it where Iris would naturally pick it up first.

With an angry exclamation the girl left the table and ran upstairs.

CHAPTER 2: THE LOCKED ROOM

Ursula Pell leaned back in her chair and shrieked with laughter.

"She *will* have stuffed dates and fancy fixin's, will she?" she cried; "I just guess she's had enough of those fallals now!"

"It quite spoiled her pretty frock," said Mrs. Bowen, timidly remonstrant.

"That's nothing, I'll buy her another. Oh, I did that pretty cleverly, I can tell you! I took a little capsule, a long, thin one, and I filled it with ink, just as you'd fill a fountain pen. Oh, oh! Iris *was* so mad! She never suspected at all; and she bit into that date—oh! oh! wasn't it funny!"

"I don't think it was," began Mrs. Bowen, but her husband lifted his eyebrows at her, and she said no more.

Though a clergyman, Alexander Bowen was not above mercenary impulses, and the mere reference, whether it had been meant or not, to a jeweled chalice made him unwilling to disapprove of anything such an influential hostess might do or say.

"Iris owes so much to her aunt," the rector said smilingly, "of course she takes such little jests in good part."

"She'd better," and Ursula Pell nodded her head; "if she knows which side her bread is buttered, she'll kiss the hand that strikes her."

"If it doesn't strike too hard," put in Mrs. Bowen, unable to resist some slight comment.

But again her husband frowned at her to keep silent, and the subject was dropped.

It was fully a quarter of an hour before Iris returned, her face red from scrubbing and still showing dark traces of the ink on chin and cheek. She wore a plain little frock of white dimity, and smiled as she resumed her seat at the table.

"Now, Aunt Ursula," she said, "if you've any more ink to spill, spill it on this dress, and not on one of my best ones."

"Fiddlestrings, Iris, I'll give you a new dress—I'll give you two. It was well worth it, to see you bite into that date! My! you looked so funny! And you look funny yet! There's ink marks all over your face!"

Mrs. Pell shook with most irritating laughter, and Iris flushed with annoyance.

"I know it, auntie; but I couldn't get them off."

"Never mind, it'll wear off in a few days. And meantime, you can wrap it up in a blotter!"

Again the speaker chuckled heartily at her own wit, and the rector joined her, while Mrs. Bowen with difficulty achieved a smile.

She was sorry for Iris, for this sort of jesting offended the girl more than it would most people, and the kind-hearted woman knew it. But, afraid of her husband's disapproval, she said nothing, and smiled, at his unspoken behest.

Nor was Iris herself entirely forgiving. One could easily see that her calmly pleasant expression covered a deeper feeling of resentment and exasperation. She had the appearance of having reached her limit, and though outwardly serene was indubitably angry.

Her pretty face, ludicrous because of the indelible smears of ink, was pale and strained, and her deep brown eyes smoldered with repressed rage. For Iris Clyde was far from meek. Her nature was, first of all, a just one, and, to a degree, retaliatory, even revengeful.

"Oh, I see your eyes snapping, Iris," exclaimed her aunt, delighted at the girl's annoyance, "I'll bet you'll get even with me for this!"

"Indeed I will, Aunt Ursula," and Iris' lips set in a straight line of determination, which, in conjunction with the ink stains, sent Mrs. Pell off into further peals of hilarity.

"Be careful, Iris," cautioned Mr. Bowen, himself wary, "if you get even with your aunt, she may leave the diamond pin to me instead of to you."

"Nixie," returned Iris saucily, "you've promised that particular diamond pin to me, haven't you, Auntie?"

"I certainly have, Iris. However often I change my will, that pin is always designated as your inheritance."

"Where is it?" asked Mr. Bowen, curiously; "may I not see it?"

"It is in a box in my lawyer's safe, at this moment," replied Mrs. Pell. "Mr. Chapin has instructions to hand the box over to Iris after my departure from this life, which I suppose you'd like to expedite, eh, Iris?"

"Well, I wouldn't go so far as to poison you," Iris smiled, "but I confess I felt almost murderous when I ran up to my room just now and looked in the mirror!"

"I don't wonder!" exclaimed Mrs. Bowen, unable to stifle her feelings longer.

"Tut! tut!" cried the rector, "what talk for Christian people!"

"Oh, they don't mean it," said Mrs. Pell, "you must take our chaff in good part, Mr. Bowen."

Dinner over, the Bowens almost immediately departed, and Iris, catching sight of her disfigured face in a mirror, turned angrily to her aunt.

"I won't stand it!" she exclaimed. "This is the last time I shall let you serve me in this fashion. I'm going to New York to-morrow, and I hope I shall never see you again!"

"Now, dearie, don't be too hard on your old auntie. It was only a joke, you know. I'll get you another frock——"

"It isn't only the frock, Aunt Ursula, it's this horrid state of things generally. Why, I never dare pick up a thing, or touch a thing—without the chance of some fool stunt making trouble for me!"

"Now, now, I will try not to do it any more. But, don't talk about going away. If you do, I'll cut you out of my will entirely."

"I don't care. That would be better than living in a trick house! Look at my face! It will be days before these stains wear off! You ought to be ashamed of yourself, Aunt Ursula!"

The old lady looked roguishly penitent, like a naughty child.

"Oh, fiddle-de-dee, you can get them off with whatcha-call-it soap. But I hope you won't! They make you look like a clown in a circus!"

Mrs. Pell's laughter had that peculiarly irritating quality that belongs to practical jokers, and Iris' sensitive nature was stung to the core.

"Oh, I hate you," she cried, "you are a fiend in human shape!" and without another word she ran upstairs to her own room.

Ursula Pell looked a little chagrined, then burst into laughter at the remembrance of Iris' face as she denounced her, and then her expression suddenly changed to one of pain, and she walked slowly to her own sitting room, went in and closed the door behind her.

It was part of the Sunday afternoon routine that Mrs. Pell should go to this room directly after dinner, and it was understood that she was not to be disturbed unless callers came.

A little later, Polly was in the dining-room arranging the sideboard, when she heard Mrs. Pell's voice. It was an agonized scream, not loud, but as one greatly frightened. The woman ran through the hall and living room to the closed door of the sitting room. Then she clearly heard her mistress calling for help.

But the door was locked on the inside, and Polly could not open it.

"Help! Thieves!" came in terrified accents, and then the voice died away to a troubled groaning; only to rise in a shrill shriek of "Help! Quickly!" and then again the moans and sighs of one in agony.

Frantically Polly hurried to the kitchen and called her husband.

"One of her damfool jokes," muttered the old man, as he shuffled toward the door of the locked room. "She's locked herself in, and she wants to get us all stirred up, thinkin' she's been attacked by thugs, an' in a minute she'll be laughin' at us."

"I don't think so," said Polly, dubiously, for she well knew her mistress' ways, "them yells was too natural."

Old Purdy listened, his ear against the door. "I can hear her rustlin' about a little," he said, "an'—there, that was a faint moan—mebbe she's been took with a spell or suthin'."

"Let's get the door open, anyway," begged Polly. "If it's a joke, I'll stand for it, but I'll bet you something's happened."

"What could happen, unless she's had a stroke, an' if that's it, she wouldn't be a callin' out 'Thieves!' Didn't you say she said that?"

"Yes, as plain as day!"

"Then that proves she's foolin' us! How could there be thieves in there, an' the door locked?"

"Well, get it open. I'm plumb scared," and Polly's round face was pale with fright.

"But I can't. Do you want me to break it in? We'd get what for in earnest if I done that!"

"Run around and look in the windows," suggested Polly, "and I'm going to call Miss Iris. I jest know something's wrong, this time."

"What is it?" asked Iris, responding to the summons, "what was that noise I heard?"

"Mrs. Pell screamed out, Miss Iris, and when I went to see what was the matter, I found the door locked, and we can't get in."

"She screamed?" said Iris. "Perhaps it's just one of her jokes."

"That's what Purdy thinks, but it didn't sound so to me. It sounded like she was in mortal danger. Here's Purdy now. Well?"

"I can't see in the windows," was his retort, "the shades is all pulled down, 'count o' the sun. She always has 'em so afternoons. And you well know, nobody could get in them windows, or out of 'em."

Ursula Pell's sitting room was also her storehouse of many treasures. Collections of curios and coins left by her husband, additional objects of value, bought by herself, made the room almost a museum; and, in addition, her desk contained money and important papers. Wherefore, she had had the windows secured by a strong steel lattice work, that made ingress impossible to marauders. Two windows faced south and two west, and there was but one door, that into the living room.

This being locked, the room was inaccessible, and the drawn shades prevented even a glimpse of the interior. The windows were open, but the shades inside the steel gratings were not to be reached.

There was no sound now from the room, and the listeners stood, looking at one another, uncertain what to do next.

"Of course it's a joke," surmised Purdy, "but even so, it's our duty to get into that room. If so be's we get laughed at for our pains, it won't be anything outa the common; and if Mrs. Pell has had a stroke—or anything has happened to her, we must see about it."

"How will you get in?" asked Iris, looking frightened.

"Bust the door down," said Purdy, succinctly. "I'll have to get Campbell to help. While I'm gone after him, you try to persuade Mrs. Pell to come out—if she's just trickin' us."

The old man went off, and Polly began to speak through the closed door.

"Let us in, Mrs. Pell," she urged. "Do, now, or Purdy'll spoil this good door. Now what's the sense o' that, if you're only a foolin'? Open the door—please do—"

But no response of any sort was made. The stillness was tragic, yet there was the possibility, even the likelihood, that the tricky mistress of the house would only laugh at them when they had forced an entrance.

"Of course it's her foolishness," said Agnes, who had joined the group. She spoke in a whisper, not wanting to brave a reprimand for impertinence. "What does she care for having a new door made, if she can get us all soured up over nothing at all?"

Iris said nothing. Only a faint, almost imperceptible tinge remained of the ink stains on her face. She had used vigorous measures, and had succeeded in removing most of the disfigurement.

Campbell returned with Purdy.

"Ah, now, Mis' Pell, come out o' there," he wheedled, "do now! It's a sin and a shame to bust in this here heavy door. Likewise it ain't no easy matter nohow. I'm not sure me and Purdy can do it. Please, Missis, unlock the door and save us all a lot of trouble."

But no sound came in answer.

"Let's all be awful still," suggested Purdy, "for quite a time, an' see if she don't make some move."

Accordingly each and every one of them scarcely breathed and the silence was intense.

"I can't hear a sound," said Campbell, at last, his ear against the keyhole, which was nearly filled by its own key. "I can't hear her breathing. You sure she's in there?"

"Of course," said Polly. "Didn't I hear her screamin'? I tell you we *got* to get in. Joke or no joke, we got to!"

"You're right," and Campbell looked serious. "I got ears like a hawk, and I bet I'd hear her breathing if she was in there. Come on, Purdy."

The door was thick and heavy, but the lock was a simple one, not a bolt, and the efforts of the two men splintered the jamb and released the door.

The sight revealed was overwhelming. The women screamed and the men stood aghast.

On the floor lay the body of Ursula Pell, and a glance was sufficient to see that she was dead. Her face was covered with blood and a small pool of it had formed near her head. Her clothing was torn and disordered, and the whole room was in a state of chaos. A table was overturned, and the beautiful lamp that had been on it, lay in shattered bits on the floor. A heavy-handled poker, belonging to the fire set, was lying near Mrs. Pell's head, and the contents of her writing-desk were scattered in mad confusion on chairs and on the floor. A secret cupboard above the mantel, really a small concealed safe, was flung open, and was empty. An empty pocket-book lay on one chair, and an empty handbag on another.

But these details were lost sight of in the attention paid to Mrs. Pell herself.

"She's dead! she's dead!" wailed Polly. "It wasn't a joke of hers—it was really robbers. She called out 'Thieves!' and 'Help!' several times. Oh, if I'd got you men in sooner!"

"But, good land, Polly!" cried Campbell, "what do you mean by thieves? How *could* anybody get in here with the door locked? Or, if he was in, how could he get out?"

"Maybe he's here now!" and Polly gazed wildly about.

"We'll soon see!" and Campbell searched the entire room. It was not difficult, for there were no alcoves or cupboards, the furniture was mostly curio cabinets, treasure tables, a few chairs and a couch. Campbell looked under the couch, and behind the window curtains, but no intruder was found.

"Mighty curious," said old Purdy, scratching his head; "how in blazes could she scream murder and thieves, when there wasn't no one in here? And how could anyone be in here with her, and get out, leavin' that 'ere door locked behind him?"

"She was murdered all right!" declared Campbell, "look at them bruises on her neck! See, her dress is tore open at the throat! What kind o' villain could 'a' done that? Gosh, it's fierce!"

Iris came timidly forward to look at the awful sight. Unable to bear it, she turned and sank on the couch, completely unnerved.

"Get a doctor, shall I?" asked Campbell, who was the most composed of them all.

"What for?" asked Purdy. "She's dead as a door nail, poor soul! But yes, I s'pose it's the proper thing. An' we oughta get the crowner, an' not touch nothin' till he comes."

"The coroner!" Iris' eyes stared at him. "What for?"

"Well, you see, Miss Iris, it's custom'ry when they's a murder——"

"But she couldn't have been murdered! Impossible! Who could have done it? It's—it's an accident."

"I wish I could think so, Miss Iris," and Purdy's honest old face was very grave, "but you look around. See, there's been robbery,—look at that there empty pocket-book an' empty bag! An' the way she's been—hit! Why, see them marks on her chest! She's fair black an' blue! And her skirt's tore—"

"Good Lord!" cried Polly, "her pocket's tore out! She always had a big pocket inside each dress skirt, and this one's been—why it's been cut out!"

There could be no doubt that the old lady had been fearfully attacked. Nor could there be any doubt of robbery. The ransacked desk, the open safe, the cut-out pocket, added to the state of the body itself, left no room for theories of accident or self-destruction.

"Holler for the doctor," commanded Purdy, instinctively taking the helm. "You telephone him, Campbell, and then he'll see about the coroner—or whoever he wants. And I think we'd oughter call up Mr. Bowen, what say, Miss Iris?"

"Mr. Bowen—why?"

"Oh, I dunno; it seems sorter decent, that's all."

"Very well, do so."

"I—I suppose I ought to telephone to Mr. Bannard——"

"Sure you ought to. But let's get the people up here first, then you can get long distance to New York afterward."

Once over the first shock of horror, Purdy's sense of responsibility asserted itself, and he was thoughtful and efficient.

"All of you go outa this room," he directed, "I'll take charge of it till the police get here. This is a mighty strange case, an' I can't see any light as to how it could 'a' happened. But it did happen—poor Mis' Pell is done for, an' I'll stand guard over her body till somebody with more authority gets here. You, Agnes, be ready to wait on the door, and Polly, you look after Miss Iris. Campbell, you telephone like I told you——"

Submissively they all obeyed him. Iris, with an effort, rose from the couch and went out to the living room. There, she sat in a big chair, and stared at nothing, until Polly, watching, became alarmed.

"Be ca'm, now, Miss Iris, do be ca'm," she urged, stupidly.

"Hush up, Polly, I am calm. Don't say such foolish things. You know I'm not the sort to faint or fly into hysterics."

"I know you ain't, Miss Iris, but you're so still and queer like——"

"Who wouldn't be? Polly, explain it. What happened to Aunt Ursula—do *you* think?"

"Miss Iris, they ain't no explanation. I'm a quick thinker, I am, and I tell you, there ain't no way that murderer—for there sure was a murderer—could 'a' got in that room or got out, with that door locked."

"Then she killed herself?"

"No, she couldn't possibly 'a' done that. You know yourself, she couldn't. When she screamed 'Thieves!' the thieves was there. Now, how did they get away? They ain't no secret way in an' out, that I know. I've lived in this house too many years to be fooled about its buildin'. It's a mystery, that's what it is, a mystery."

"Will it ever be solved?" and Iris looked at old Polly as if inquiring of a sibyl.

"Land, child, how do I know? I ain't no seer. I s'pose some of those smart detectives can make it out, but it's beyond me!"

"Oh, Polly, they won't have detectives, will they?"

"Sure they will, Miss Iris; they'll have to."

"Now, I'm through with the telephone," said Campbell, reappearing. "Shall I get New York for you, Miss?"

"No," said Iris, rising, "I'll get the call myself."

CHAPTER 3: THE EVIDENCE OF THE CHECKBOOK

Winston Bannard's apartments in New York were comfortable though not luxurious. The Caxton Annex catered to young bachelors who were not millionaires but who liked to live pleasantly, and Bannard had been contentedly ensconced there ever since he had left his aunt's home.

He had always been glad he had made the move, for the city life was far more to his liking than the village ways of Berrien, and if his law practice could not be called enormous, it was growing and he had developed some real ability.

Of late he had fallen in with a crowd of men much richer than himself, and association with them had led to extravagance in the matter of cards for high stakes, motors of high cost, and high living generally.

The high cost of living is undeniable, and Bannard not infrequently found himself in financial difficulties of more or less depth and importance.

As he entered his rooms Sunday evening about seven, he found a telegram and a telephone notice from the hotel office. The latter merely informed him that Berrien, Connecticut, had called him at four o'clock. The telegram read:

"For Heaven's sake come up here at once. Aunt Ursula is dead."

It was signed Iris, and Bannard read it, standing by the window to catch the gleams of fading daylight. Then he sank into a chair, and read it over again, though he now knew it by rote.

He was not at all stunned. His alert mind traveled quickly from one thought to another, and for ten minutes his tense, strained position, his set jaw and his occasionally winking eyes betokened successive cogitations on matters of vital importance.

Then he jumped up, looked at his watch, consulted a time-table, and, not waiting for an elevator, ran down the stairs through that atmosphere of Sunday afternoon quiet, which is perhaps nowhere more noticeable than in a city hotel.

A taxicab, a barely caught train, and before nine o'clock Winston Bannard was at the Berrien railroad station.

Campbell was there to meet him, and as they drove to the house Bannard sat beside the chauffeur that he might learn details of the tragedy.

"But I don't understand, Campbell," Bannard said, "how could she be murdered, alone in her room, with the door locked? Did she—didn't she—kill herself?"

But the chauffeur was close-mouthed. "I don't know, Mr. Bannard," he returned, "it's all mighty queer, and the detective told me not to gossip or chatter about it at all."

"But, my stars! man, it isn't gossip to tell *me* all there is to tell."

"But there's nothing to tell. The bare facts you know— I've told you those; as to the rest, the police or Miss Iris must tell you."

"You're right," agreed Bannard. "I'm glad you are not inclined to guess or surmise. There must be some explanation, of course. How about the windows?"

"Well, you know those windows, Mr. Bannard. They're as securely barred as the ones in the bank, and more so. Ever since Mrs. Pell took that room for her treasure room, about eight or ten years ago, they've been protected by steel lattice work and that's untouched. That settles the windows, and there's only the one door, and that Purdy and I broke open. Now, that's all I know about it."

Bannard relapsed into silence, and Campbell didn't speak again until they reached the house.

"Oh, I'm so glad you've come!" was the first greeting to the young man as he entered the hall at Pellbrook. It was spoken by Mrs. Bowen, who had been with Iris ever since she was summoned by telephone, that afternoon. "It's all so dreadful,—the doctors are examining the body now— and the coroner is here—and two detectives—and Iris is so queer——" the poor little lady quite broke down, in her relief at having some one to share her responsibility.

"Isn't Mr. Bowen here?" Bannard said, as he followed her into the living-room.

"No, he had to attend service, he'll come after church. Here is Iris."

The girl did not rise at Bannard's approach, but sat, looking up at him, her face full of inquiry.

"Where have you been?" she demanded; "why didn't you come sooner? I telegraphed at four o'clock—I telephoned first, but they said—they said you were out."

"I was; I only came in at seven, and then I found your messages, and I caught the first train possible."

"It doesn't matter," said Iris, wearily. "There's nothing you can do—nothing anybody can do. Oh, Win, it's horrible!"

"Of course it is, Iris. But I'm so in the dark. Tell me all about it."

"Oh, I can't. I can't seem to talk about it. Mrs. Bowen will tell you."

The little lady told all she knew, and then, one of the detectives appeared to question Bannard. He explained his presence and told who he was and then asked to go into his aunt's sitting room.

"Not just now," said the man, whose name was Hughes, "the doctors are busy in there, with the coroner."

"Why so late," asked Bannard; "what have they been doing all the afternoon?"

"Doctor Littell came at once," explained Mrs. Bowen, "he's her own doctor, you know. But that coroner, Doctor Timken, never got here till this evening. Why, here's Mr. Chapin!"

Charles Chapin, who was Mrs. Pell's lawyer, entered, and also Mr. Bowen, so there was quite a group in waiting when the doctors came out of the closed room.

"It's the strangest case imaginable," said Coroner Timken, his face white and terrified. "There's not the least possibility of suicide—and yet there's no explanation for a murder."

"Why do you say that?" asked Chapin, who had heard little of the details.

"The body is terribly injured. There are livid bruises on her chest, shoulders and upper arms. There are marks on her wrists, as if she had been bound by ropes, and similar marks on her ankles."

"Incredible!" cried Mr. Chapin. "Bound?"

"The marks can mean nothing else. They are as if cords had been tightly drawn, and on one ankle the stocking is slightly stained with blood."

"What?" exclaimed Mrs. Bowen.

"Yes, and the flesh beneath the stain is abraded round the ankle, and the skin broken. The other ankle shows slight marks of the cord, but it did not cut into the flesh on that side. Her wrists, too, show red marks and indentations, as of cords. It is inexplicable."

"But the bruises?" pursued Mr. Chapin, "and the awful wound on her face?"

"There is no doubt that she was attacked for the purpose of robbery. Moreover, the thief was looking for something in particular. It is clear that he stole money or valuables, but the state of the desk and safe prove a desperate hunt for some paper or article of special value. Also the pocket, cut and torn from the skirt, proves a determination to secure the treasure. As we reconstruct the crime, the intruder intimidated Mrs. Pell by threats and by physical violence; tied her while search was made through her room; and then, in a rage of disappointment, flung the old lady to the floor, where she hit her head on a sharp-pointed brass knob of the fender. This penetrated her temple and caused her death. These things are facts;

also the state of the room, the overturned table and chairs, the broken lamp, the ransacked desk and safe—all these are facts; but what theory can account for the disappearance of the murderer from the locked room?"

There was no answer until Detective Hughes said, "I've always been told that the more mysterious and insoluble a crime seems to be, the easier it is to solve it."

"You have, eh?" returned the coroner; "then get busy on this one. It's beyond me. Why, that woman's wrist is sprained, if not broken, she has some internal injuries and she was suffering from shock and fright. The attack was diabolical! It may be that the murder was unpremeditated, but the mauling and bruising of the old lady was the work of a strong man and a hardened wretch."

"Why didn't she scream sooner?" asked Hughes, who was listening intently. He had been detailed on other duties while his confreres investigated the scene of the crime.

"Gagged, probably," answered Timken. "There are slight marks at the corners of her mouth which indicate a gag was used, for a time at least. How long was it," he said abruptly, turning to Iris, "that your aunt was in that room alone? I mean alone, so far as you knew?"

"I don't know; I was up in my own room all the time after dinner, and—I don't know what time it was when they called me—I seem to have lost all track of time——"

"Don't bother the girl," said Mrs. Bowen. "Polly, you tell about the time."

The servants were in and out of the room, now clustered at the doorway, now hurrying off on errands and back again.

"It musta been about ha' past three when I heard her scream," said Polly, "or maybe a bit earlier, but not much. I was in the dining room, settin' the sideboard to rights after dinner, and I heard her holler."

"And you went to the door at once?"

"Yes; just 's quick 's I could. But the door was locked——"

"Was that usual?"

"Yes, sir, she often locks it when she takes a nap Sunday afternoons. And then I went and called Purdy, and we couldn't get in."

"Yes, I know about the barred windows and so on. Did you hear any further sounds from Mrs. Pell?"

"Some; sorta movin' around an' faint moanin's. But the truth is—we thought she was a foolin' us."

"Fooling you?"

"Yes, sir. Mrs. Pell, she was great for jokin'. Many's the time she's hollered, 'Help! Polly!' and when I'd get there, she'd laugh fit to kill at me. She was that way, sir. She was always foolin' us."

"Is this true?" asked Timken, turning to the others.

They all corroborated Polly's statements. Even Chapin, the lawyer, told of jests and tricks his wealthy client had played on him, and Winston Bannard declared he had suffered so much from his aunt's whims that he had been forced to move away.

"And you, Miss Clyde, did she so tease you?"

"Indeed she did," said Iris. "I think I was her favorite victim. Scarcely a day passed that she did not annoy and distress me by some practical joke. You know about the ink, this noon——" she turned to Mrs. Bowen.

"Yes," said that lady, but she looked grave and thoughtful.

"But surely," pursued the coroner, "one could tell the difference between the screams of a victim in mortal agony, and those of a jest!"

"No, sir," and Polly shook her head. "Mrs. Pell was that clever, she'd make you think she'd been hurt awful, when she was just trickin' you. But, any ways, sir, me an' Purdy we did all we could, and we couldn't get in. Then Campbell, he come, and helped to break down the door——"

"And you're sure the murderer couldn't have slipped through as you opened the door?"

"Not a chance!" spoke up Campbell. "We smashed it open, the lock just splintered out of the jamb, as you can see for yourself, and we were all gathered in a clump on this side. No, sir, the room was quiet as death—and empty, save for Mrs. Pell, herself."

"And she was dead, then?"

"Yes, sir," asseverated Purdy, solemnly. "I ain't no doctor, but I made sure she was dead. She'd died within a minute or so, she was most as warm as in life, and the blood was still a flowin' from her head where she was struck."

"Did you move anything in the room?"

"No, sir, only so much as was necessary to get around. The table that was upset had a 'lectric lamp on it, which had a long danglin' green cord, 'cause it was put in after the reg'lar wirin' was done. I coiled up that 'ere cord, and picked up the pieces of broken glass, so's we could step around. But I left the bag and pocket-book and all, just where they was flung. And the litter from the desk, all over the floor, I didn't touch that, neither—nor I didn't touch the body."

Purdy's voice faltered and his old eyes filled with tears.

"You did well," commended the coroner, nodding his head kindly at him, "just one more question. Was Mrs. Pell in her usual good spirits yesterday? Did she do anything or say anything that seemed out of the ordinary?"

"No," and Purdy shook his head. "I don't think so, do you, Polly?"

"Not that I noticed," said his wife. "She cut up an awful trick on Miss Iris, but that wasn't to say unusual."

"What was it?" and the coroner listened to an account of the date with ink in it. The story was told by Mrs. Bowen, as Iris refused to talk at all.

"A pretty mean trick," was the coroner's opinion. "Didn't you resent it, Miss Clyde?"

"She did not," spoke up the rector, in a decided way. "Miss Clyde is a young woman of too much sense and also of too much affection for her dear aunt, to resent a good-humored jest——"

"Good-humored jest!" exclaimed Hughes. "Going some! a jest like that—spoilin' a young girl's pretty Sunday frock——"

"Never mind, Hughes," reproved Timken, "we're not judging Mrs. Pell's conduct now. This is an investigation, a preliminary inquiry, rather, but not a judgment seat. Miss Clyde, I must ask that you answer me a few questions. You left your aunt's presence directly after your guests had departed?"

"Within a few moments of their leaving."

"She was then in her usual health and good spirits?"

"So far as I know."

"Any conversation passed between you?'

"Only a little."

"Amicable?'

"What do you mean by that?"

"Friendly—affectionate—not quarrelsome."

"It was not exactly affectionate, as I told her I was displeased at her spoiling my gown."

"Ah. And what did she say?"

"That she would buy me another."

"Did that content you?"

"I wasn't discontented. I was annoyed at her unkind trick, and I told her so. That is all."

"Of course that is all," again interrupted Mr. Bowen. "I can answer for the cordial relationship between aunt and niece and I can vouch for the fact that these merry jests didn't really stir up dissension between these two estimable people. Why, only to-day, Mrs. Pell was dilating on the wonderful legacies she meant to bestow on Miss Clyde. She also referred to a jeweled chalice for my church, but I am sure these remarks were in no way prompted by any thought of immediate death. On the contrary, she was in gayer spirits than I have ever seen her."

"I think she was over-excited," said Mrs. Bowen, thoughtfully. "Don't you, Iris? She was giggling in an almost hysterical manner, it seemed to me."

"I didn't notice," said Iris, wearily. "Aunt Ursula was a creature of moods. She was grave or gay without apparent reason. I put up with her silly jokes usually, but to-day's performance seemed unnecessary and unkind. However, it doesn't matter now."

"No," declared Winston Bannard, "and it does no good to rake over the old lady's queer ways. We all know about her habit of playing tricks, and I, for one, don't wonder that Polly thought she screamed out to trick somebody. Nor does it matter. If Polly hadn't thought that, she couldn't have done any more than she did do to get into that room as soon as possible. Could she, now?"

"No," agreed the coroner. "Nor does it really affect our problem of how the murder was committed."

"Let me have a look into that room," said Bannard, suddenly.

"You a detective?" asked Timken.

"Not a bit of it, but I want to see its condition."

"Come on in," said the other. "They've put Mrs. Pell's body on the couch, but, except for that, nothing's been touched."

Hughes went in with Bannard and the coroner, and the three men were joined by Lawyer Chapin.

Silently they took in the details. The still figure on the couch, with face solemnly covered, seemed to make conversation undesirable.

Hughes alertly moved about peering at things but touching almost nothing. Bannard and Mr. Chapin stood motionless gazing at the evidences of crime.

"Got a cigarette?" whispered Hughes to Bannard and mechanically the young man took out his case and offered it. The detective took one and then continued his minute examination of the room and its appointments.

At last he sat down in front of the desk and began to look through such papers as remained in place. There were many pigeonholes and compartments, which held small memorandum books and old letters and stationery.

Hughes opened and closed several books, and then suddenly turned to Bannard with this question.

"You haven't been up here to-day, have you, Mr. Bannard? I mean, before you came up this evening."

"N-no, certainly not," was the answer, and the man looked decidedly annoyed. "What are you getting at, Mr. Hughes?"

"Oh, nothing. Where have you been all day, Mr. Bannard?"

"In New York city.'

"Not been out of it?"

"I went out this morning for a bicycle ride, my favorite form of exercise. Am I being quizzed?"

"You are. You state that you were not up here, in this room, this afternoon, about three o'clock?"

"I certainly do affirm that! Why?"

"Because I observe here on the desk a half-smoked cigarette of the same kind you just gave me.

"And you think that is incriminating evidence! A little far-fetched, Mr. Hughes."

"Also, on this chair is a New York paper of to-day's date, and not the one that is usually taken in this house."

"Indeed!" but Winston Bannard had turned pale.

"And," continued Hughes, holding up a check-book, "this last stub in Mrs. Pell's check-book shows that she made out to *you to-day*, a check for five thousand dollars!"

"What!" cried Mr. Chapin.

"Yes, sir, a check stub, in Mrs. Pell's own writing, dated *to-day*! Where is that check, Mr. Winston Bannard, and when did you get it? And why did you kill your aunt afterward? What were you searching this room for? Come, sir, speak up!"

CHAPTER 4: TIMKEN AND HIS INQUIRIES

"You must be out of your mind, Mr. Hughes," said Bannard; but, as a matter of fact, he looked more as if he himself were demented. His face wore a wild, frightened expression, and his fingers twitched nervously, as he picked at the edge of his coat. "Of course, I haven't been up here to-day, before I came this evening. That *New York Herald* was never in my possession. Because I live in New York City, I'm not the only one who reads the 'Herald.'"

"But your aunt subscribed only to *The Times*. Where did that 'Herald' come from?"

"I'm sure I don't know. It must have been left here by somebody—I suppose——"

"And this half-burnt cigarette, of the same brand as those you have in your pocket case?"

"Other men smoke those, too, I assume."

"Well, then, the check, which this stub shows to have been drawn to-day to you. Where is that?"

"Not in my possession. If my aunt made that out to me it was doubtless for a present and she may have sent it to me in a letter; in which case it will reach my city address to-morrow morning, or she may have put it somewhere up here for safe keeping."

"All most unlikely," said Mr. Chapin, shaking his head. "Did Mrs. Pell send any letters to the post-office to-day, does any one know?"

Campbell was called, and he said that his mistress had given him a number of letters to mail when he took Miss Clyde to church that morning.

"Was one of them directed to Mr. Bannard," asked Hughes.

"How should I know?" said the chauffeur, turning red.

"Oh, it's no crime to glance at the addresses on envelopes," said Hughes, encouragingly. "Curiosity may not be an admirable trait, but it isn't against the law. And it will help us a lot if you can answer my question."

"Then, no, sir, there wasn't," and Campbell looked ashamed but positive.

"And there was no other chance for Mrs. Pell to mail a letter to-day?" went on Hughes.

"No, sir; none of us has been to the village since, and the post-office closes at noon on Sunday anyhow."

"All that proves nothing," said Bannard, impatiently. "If my aunt drew that check to me it is probably still in this room somewhere, and if not it is quite likely she destroyed it, in a sudden change of mind. She has done that before, in my very presence. You know, Mr. Chapin, how uncertain her decisions are."

"That's true," the lawyer agreed, "I've drawn up papers for her often, only to have her tear them up before my very eyes, and demand a document of exactly opposite intent."

"So, you see," insisted Bannard, who had regained his composure, "that check means nothing, the New York newspaper is not incriminating and the cigarette is not enough to prove my guilty presence at the time of this crime. Unless the police force of Berrien can do better than that, I suggest getting a worthwhile detective from the city."

Hughes looked angrily at the speaker, but said nothing.

"That is not a bad suggestion," said Chapin. "This is a big crime and a most mysterious one. It involves the large fortune of Mrs. Pell, which, I happen to know, was mostly invested in jewels. These gems she has so secretly and securely hidden that even I have not the remotest idea where they are. Is it not conceivable that they were in that wall-safe, and have been stolen by the murderer?"

"Good Lord!" exclaimed Hughes. "I didn't know she kept her fortune here!"

"Nor do I know it," returned Chapin. "But, doubtless, something of value was in that safe, now empty, and I only surmise that it may have been her great collection of precious stones."

"Have you her will?" asked Bannard, abruptly.

"Yes, her latest one," replied Chapin. "You know she made a new one on the average of once a month or so."

"Who inherits?"

"I don't know. A box, bequeathed to Miss Clyde and a—something similar to you, probably contain her principal bequests. This house, however, she has left to another relative, and there are other bequests. I do not deny the will is that of an eccentric woman, as will be shown at its reading, in due time."

"That's all right," broke in the coroner, "but what I'm interested in is catching the murderer."

"And solving the mystery of his getting in," supplemented Hughes.

"She might have let him in," assumed Timken.

"All right, but how did he get out?"

"That's the mystery," mused Chapin. "I can see no light on that question, whatever, can you, Winston?"

"No," said Bannard, shortly. "There's no secret entrance to this room, of that I'm positive. And with the windows barred, and those people at the door, as it was broken open, there seems no explanation."

"Oh, pshaw," said Timken, "that's all for future consideration. The lady couldn't have killed herself. Somebody got in and the same somebody got out. It's up to the detectives to find out how. If a human being could do it, and did do it, another human being can find out how. But let us get at the possible criminal. Motive is the first consideration."

"The heirs are always looked upon as having motive," said Lawyer Chapin, "but, in this case, I feel sure the principal heirs are Miss Clyde and Mr. Bannard, and I cannot suspect either of them."

"Iris—ridiculous!" exclaimed Bannard. "For Heaven's sake, don't drag her name in!"

"Where is Miss Clyde's bedroom?" asked Hughes, suddenly.

"Directly above this room," returned Bannard. "Are you going to suggest that she came down here by a concealed staircase, and maltreated her aunt in this ferocious manner? Mr. Hughes, do confine yourself to theories that at least have a slight claim to common sense!"

And yet, when the coroner held his inquest next day, more than one who listened to the evidence leaned toward the suggestion of Iris Clyde's possible connection with the crime.

The girl's own manner was against her, or rather against her chance of gaining the sympathies of the audience.

The inquest was held in Pellbrook. The big living room was filled with interested listeners, who also crowded the hall, and drifted into the dining room. The room where Mrs. Pell had died was closed to all, but curiosity-seekers hovered around it outside, and inspected the steel protected windows, and discoursed wisely of secret passages and concealed exits.

As the one known to have last spoken with her aunt, Iris was closely questioned. But her replies were of no help in getting at the truth. She admitted that she and her aunt quarreled often, and agreed that that was the real reason she had decided to go to New York to live.

But her answers were curt, even angry at times, and her manner was haughty and resentful.

Great emphasis was laid by the coroner on the tenor of the last words that passed between Iris and her aunt.

The girl admitted that they were quarrelsome words, but declared she did not remember exactly what had been said.

Something in the expression of the maid, Agnes, caught the eye of the coroner, and he suddenly turned to her, saying, "Did you overhear this conversation?"

Taken aback by the unexpected question, Agnes stammered, "Yes, sir, I did."

"Where were you?"

"In the dining room, clearing the table."

"Where was Miss Clyde?"

"In the hall, just about to go upstairs."

"And Mrs. Pell?"

"In the hall, by the living-room door."

"Why were they in the hall?"

"Mr. and Mrs. Bowen had just left, and the ladies had said good-bye to them at the front door, and then they stood talking to each other a few moments."

"What were they talking about?"

Agnes hesitated, but on further insistence of the coroner she said, "Miss Iris was complaining to Mrs. Pell about her habit of playing tricks."

"Was Miss Clyde angry at her aunt?"

"She sounded so."

"Certainly I was," broke in Iris. "I had stood that foolishness just as long as I could——"

"You are not the witness, for the moment, Miss Clyde," said the coroner, severely. "Agnes, what did Mrs. Pell say to her niece in response to her chiding?"

"She only laughed, and said that Miss Iris looked like a circus clown."

"Then what did Miss Clyde say?"

"She said that Mrs. Pell was a fiend in human shape and that she hated her. Then she ran upstairs and went into her own room and slammed the door."

"Have you any reason to think, Agnes, that there is any secret mode of connection between Mrs. Pell's sitting room and Miss Clyde's bedroom, directly above it?"

"Why, no, sir, I never heard of such a thing."

"Absurd!" broke in Winston Bannard, "utterly absurd. If there were such a thing, it could certainly be discovered by your expert detectives."

"There isn't any," declared Hughes, positively. "I've sounded the walls and examined the floor and ceiling, and there's not a chance of it. The way the murderer got out of that locked room is a profound mystery, but it won't be solved by means of a secret entrance."

"Yet what other possibility can be suggested?" went on Timken, thoughtfully. "And the connection needn't be directly with Miss Clyde's room. Suppose there is a sliding wall panel, or an exit to the cellar, in some way."

"But there isn't," insisted Hughes. "I'm not altogether ignorant of architecture, and there is no such thing in any part of that room. Moreover, how could any outsider come to the house, get in, and get into that room, without any member of the household seeing his approach? The two women servants were in the house, but Campbell, the chauffeur, and Purdy, the gardener, were out of doors, and could have seen anyone who came in at the gate."

"Might not the intruder have entered while the family was at dinner, and concealed himself in Mrs. Pell's sitting room, until she went in there after dinner?"

"Possibly," agreed Hughes, "but, in that case, how did the intruder get out?"

And that was the sticking-point with every theory. No one could think of or imagine any way to account for the exit of the criminal. Mrs. Pell had undoubtedly been murdered. Her injuries were not self-inflicted. She had been brutally maltreated by a strong, angry person, before the final blow had killed her. The overturned table, and the ransacked room, the empty pocket-book and handbag were the work of a desperate thief, and it really seemed absurd to connect the name of Iris Clyde with such conditions. More plausible was the theory of Bannard's guilt, but, again, how did he get away?

"There is a possibility of locking a door from the outside," said Coroner Timken.

"I've thought of that," returned Hughes, "but it wasn't done in this case. I've tried to lock that door from outside, with a pair of nippers, and the lock is such that it can't be done. And, too, Polly heard Mrs. Pell's screams at the moment of her murder—the criminal couldn't have run out, and locked the door outside, and gone through this room without having been seen by someone. You were in the dining room, Polly?"

"Yes, sir, and I ran right in here; there was no time for anybody to get away without my seeing him."

The facts, as testified to, were so clear cut and definite, that there seemed little to probe into. It was a deadlock. Mrs. Pell had been robbed and murdered. Apparently there was no way in which this could have been done, and yet it had been done. The two who could be said to have a motive were Iris Clyde and Winston Bannard. It might even be said that they had opportunity, yet it was clearly shown that they could not have escaped unseen.

Bannard was further questioned as to his movements on Sunday.

He declared that he had risen late, and had gone for a bicycle ride, a recreation of which he was fond.

"Where did you ride?" asked Timken.

"Up Broadway and on along its continuation as far as Red Fox Inn."

"That's about half way up here!"

"I know it. I stopped there for luncheon, about noon, and after that I returned to New York."

"You lunched at the Inn at noon?"

"Shortly after twelve, I think it was. The Inn people will verify this."

"They know you?"

"Not personally, but doubtless the waiter who served me will remember my presence."

"And, after luncheon, you returned to the city?"

"I did."

"Reaching your home at what time?"

"Oh, I didn't go to my rooms until about twilight. It was a lovely day, and I came home slowly, stopping here and there when I passed a bit of woods or a pleasant spot to rest. I often spend a day in the open."

"You had your newspaper with you?"

"I did."

"What one?"

"The 'Herald.'" But even as Bannard said the words, he caught himself, and looked positively frightened.

"Ah, yes. There is even now a 'Herald' of yesterday's date in Mrs. Pell's sitting room."

"But that isn't mine. That—that one isn't unfolded—I mean, it hasn't been unfolded. You can see that by its condition. Mine, I read through, and refolded it untidily, even inside out."

"Fine talk!" said Timken, with a slight sneer. "But it doesn't get you anywhere. That New York paper, that cigarette end, and that check stub seem to me to need pretty strict accounting for. Your explanations are glib, but a little thin. I don't see how you got out of the room, or Miss Clyde either; but that consideration would apply equally to any other intruder. And we have no other direction in which to look for the person who robbed Mrs. Pell."

"Leave Miss Clyde's name out," said Bannard, shortly. "If you want to suspect me, go ahead, but it's too absurd to fasten it on a woman."

"Perhaps you both know more than you've told——"

"I don't!" declared Iris, her eyes snapping at the implication. "I was angry at my aunt. I've told you the truth about that, but I didn't kill her. Nor did her nephew. Because we are her probable heirs does not mean that we're her murderers!"

"Your protestation doesn't carry much weight," said Timken, coldly. "We're after proofs, and we'll get them yet. Mr. Bowen, will you take the stand?"

The rector somewhat ponderously acquiesced, and the coroner put some questions to him, which like the preceding queries brought little new light on the mystery.

But one statement roused a slight wave of suspicion toward Iris Clyde. This was the assertion that Mrs. Pell had said she would call her lawyer to her the next day, to change her will.

"With what intent?" asked Timken.

"She promised that she would have all her jewels set into a chalice, and present it to me for my church."

"Oh, she didn't mean that, Mr. Bowen," Iris exclaimed.

"Why didn't she? She said it, and I have no reason to think she was not sincere."

"She may have meant it when she said it," put in Lawyer Chapin, "but she was likely to change her mind before she changed her will."

"That's mere supposition on your part," objected Mr. Bowen.

"But I know my late client better than you do. She changed her will frequently, but her fortune was always left to her relatives, not to any institution or charity."

"She said that she had never thought of it before," Mr. Bowen related, "but that she considered it a fine idea."

"Oh, then you proposed it?" said Timken.

"Yes, I did," replied the clergyman, "I suggested it half jestingly, but when Mrs. Pell acquiesced with evident gladness, I certainly hoped she would put at least part of her fortune into such a good cause."

"You heard this discussion, Miss Clyde?" asked the coroner.

"Of course I did; it occurred at the dinner table."

"And were you not afraid your aunt would make good her promise?"

"She didn't really promise——"

"Afraid then that she would carry out the minister's suggestion."

"I didn't really think much about it. If you mean, did I kill her to prevent such a possibility, I answer I certainly did not!"

And so the futile inquiry went on. Nobody could offer any evidence that pointed toward a solution of the mysterious murder. Nobody could fasten the crime on anyone, or even hint a suggestion of which way to look for the criminal.

Sam Torrey, a brother of Agnes, the maid, testified that he had seen a strange man prowling round the Pell house Sunday morning, but as the lad was reputed to be of a defective mind, and as the tragedy occurred on Sunday afternoon, little attention was paid to him.

Roger Downing, a young man of the village, said he saw a stranger near Pellbrook about noon. But this, too, meant nothing.

No testimony mentioned a stranger or any intruder near the Pell place in the afternoon. The Bowens had left the house at about three, and Polly heard her mistress scream less than half an hour later. No one could fix the time exactly, but it was assumed to be about twenty or twenty-five minutes past the hour.

This meant, the coroner pointed out, that the murderer acted rapidly; for to upset the room as he had done, while the mistress of the house was bound and gagged, watching him; then afterward—as Timken reconstructed the crime—to torture the poor woman in his efforts to find the jewels or whatever he was after; and then, in a final frenzy of hatred, to dash her to the floor and kill her by knocking her head on the point of the fender, all meant the desperate, speedy work of a double-dyed villain. As to his immediate disappearance, which took place between the time when he dashed her to the floor and when Purdy broke in the door, the coroner was unable to offer any explanation whatever.

CHAPTER 5: DOWNING'S EVIDENCE

And so the case went to the coroner's jury. And after some discussion they returned the inevitable verdict of murder by person or persons unknown. Some of them preferred the phrase, "causes unknown." But others pointed out that the physical causes of Mrs. Pell's death were only too evident; the question was: Who was the perpetrator of the ghastly deed?

And so the foreman somewhat importantly announced that the deceased met her death at the hands of persons unknown, and in most mysterious and inexplicable circumstances, but recommended that every possible effort be made to trace any connection that might exist between the tragedy and the heirs to the fortune of the deceased.

A distinct murmur of disapproval sounded through the room, yet there were those who wagged assenting heads.

The inquest had been a haphazard affair in some ways. Berrien was possessed of only a limited police force, and its head, Inspector Clare, was a man whose knowledge of police matters consisted of an education beyond his intelligence. Moreover, the case itself was so weirdly tragic, so out of all reason or belief, that the whole force was at its wits' end. The bluecoats at the doors of Pellbrook were as interested in the village gossip as the villagers themselves. And though entrance was made difficult, most of the influential members of the community were assembled to hear the inquiry into this strange matter.

There were so few material witnesses, those who were questioned knew so little, and, more than all, the mystery of the murder in the locked room was so baffling, that there was, of course, no possibility of other than an open verdict.

"It's all very well," said the inspector, pompously, "to bring in that verdict. Yes, that's all very well. But the murderers must be found. A crime like this must not go unpunished. It's mysterious, of course, but the truth must be ferreted out. We're only at the beginning. There is much to be learned beside the meager evidence we have already collected."

The mass of people had broken up into small groups, all of whom were confabbing with energy. There were several strangers present, for the startling details of the case, as reported in the city papers, had brought a number of curious visitors from the metropolis.

One of these, a quiet-mannered, middle-aged man, edged nearer to where the inspector was talking to Bannard and Iris Clyde. Hughes was listening, also Mr. Bowen and Mr. Chapin.

"It's this way," the inspector was saying, in his unpolished manner of speech, "we've got her alive at three, talking to her niece, and we've got her dying at half-past three, and calling for help. Between these two stated times, the murderer attacked her, manhandled her pretty severely and flung her down to her death, besides ransacking the room, and stealing nobody knows what or how much. Seems to me a remarkable affair like that ought to be easier to get at than a simple everyday robbery."

"It ought to be, I think, too," said the stranger, in a mild, pleasant voice. "May I ask how you're going about it?"

"Who are you, sir?" asked Clare. "You got any right here? A reporter?"

"No, not a reporter. An humble citizen of New York city, not connected with the police force in any way. But I'm interested in this mystery, and I judge you have in mind some definite plan to work on."

Mollified, even flattered at the man's evident faith in him, the inspector replied, "Yes, sir, yes, I may say I have. Perhaps not for immediate disclosure, no, not that, but I have a pretty strong belief that we'll yet round up the villains——"

"You assume more than one person, then?"

"I think so, yes, I may say I think so. But that's of little moment. If we can run down the clues we have, if we can follow their pointing fingers, we shall know the criminal, and learn whether or not he had accomplices in his vile work."

"Quite so," and with a smile and a nod, the stranger drifted away.

Another man came near, then, and frankly introduced himself as Joe Young, from a nearby town, saying he wanted to be allowed to examine the wall-safe said to have been rifled by the murderer.

"My father built that safe," he explained his interest, "and I think it might lead to some further enlightenment."

Detective Hughes accompanied Young to the closed room that had been Mrs. Pell's sanctum, and they entered alone.

"Don't touch things," cautioned Hughes. "I've not really had a chance yet to go over the place with a fine tooth comb. They've taken the poor lady's body away, but otherwise nothing's been touched——"

"Oh, I won't touch anything," agreed Young, "but I couldn't help a sort of a notion that my father might have built more than a safe—he was a skilful carpenter and joiner, and Mrs. Pell was a tricky woman. I mean by that, she was mighty fond of tricking people and she easily could have had a secret cupboard, or even an entrance from somewhere behind that safe."

But no amount of searching could discover the slightest possibility of such a thing. The open safe was an ordinary, built-in-the-wall affair, not large enough to suggest an entrance for a person. Nor was there any secret compartment behind it or anything other than showed on the surface. The door, when closed, had been covered by a picture, which had been taken down and flung on the floor. The safe was absolutely empty, and no one knew what it had contained.

Young was decidedly disappointed. "I had no personal motive in looking this thing up," he said, "I only hoped that my knowledge of my father's clever work might lead to some discovery that would prove helpful to you detectives or to the family. But it's plain to be seen there's no hocus-pocus about this thing. It's as simple a safe as I ever saw. Nothing, in fact, but a concealed cupboard with a combination lock. Wonder who opened it? The murderer?"

"I don't think so," rejoined Hughes. "I think the intruder, whoever he was, compelled the old lady to open it for him."

"You stick to the masculine gender, I see, in your assumptions."

"I do. I don't think for a minute that Miss Clyde is involved."

"But her room is just above this——"

"Oh, that's what you're after! A secret connection between this room and Miss Clyde's by way of the safe!"

"Yes, that's what I had in mind. But there's not the slightest possibility of it, is there?"

"No, nor any other secret passage of any sort or kind. Oh, I've investigated fully in that respect. I meant, I haven't searched for tiny clues and little scraps of evidence. Straws, in fact, do show which way the wind blows."

"Well, I don't suppose I can be of any help, but if I can, call on me. I live in East Fallville, only twelve miles away, and I'd like nothing better than to dig into this mystery, if I'm wanted."

"Thank you, Mr. Young, I appreciate your helpful spirit, and I'll call on you if it's available. But I don't mind owning up that we have more people to look into this matter than directions in which to look. As you may imagine, it's a baffling thing to get hold of. I confess I hardly know which way to turn."

As the two men returned to the living room, Hughes overheard some angry words between Bannard and Roger Downing, one of the dwellers in the village.

"But I saw you," Downing was saying.

"You think you did," returned Bannard, "but you're mistaken."

"When?" asked Hughes, suddenly and sharply, of Downing.

"Sunday about noon. Win Bannard was skulking around in the woods just back of this house——"

"Skulking! Take back that word!" cried Bannard.

"Well, you were sauntering around, then, dawdling around, whatever you want it called, but you were there!"

"I was not," declared Bannard.

"And I saw your little motor car waiting for you a bit farther along the road——"

"You did!" and Bannard laughed shortly, "well, as it happens I don't own a motor car!"

"Nonsense, Roger," said Hughes, "Win Bannard wasn't up here Sunday noon—where would he have been concealed until three o'clock——"

"In his aunt's room——"

"Take that back!" shouted Bannard, "do you know what you're saying?"

"Hush up, both of you," cautioned Hughes. "For Heaven's sake don't get up a scene over nothing! But, if you saw a small motor car along the road near here, I want to know about it. What time was this, Downing?"

"'Long about noon, I tell you," was the sulky reply. "It might have been a few minutes before. There was no one in the car; it was drawn up by the side of the road, not more'n two hundred yards from the house."

"And you thought you saw Mr. Bannard. Of course, it was someone else, but it's important to know about this. I can't help thinking whoever committed that murder was hidden in the room for some time beforehand——"

"And how did he get away?" asked Bannard.

"If you ask me that once more, I'll pound you! I don't *know* how he got away. But he did get away, and we'll find out how, when we find our man. That's my theory of procedure, if you want to know; let the mystery of the locked room wait, and devote all possible effort to finding the murderer. Then the rest will unravel itself."

"Easier said than done," sneered Downing, "if you're going to discard all evidence or statements that anyone makes to you!"

"If you were so sure you saw Mr. Bannard on Sunday morning, why didn't you so state at the inquest?"

"I wasn't asked, and besides 'twas about noon, and old Timken only asked about the afternoon——"

"And besides," broke in Bannard, "you weren't sure you did see me, and you weren't sure you saw anybody, and you made up this whole yarn, anyhow!"

"Nothing of the sort, and you'll find out, Win Bannard, when I tell all I know——"

"Quit it now," ordered Hughes; "if you've anything to tell of real importance, Roger, tell it to me when we're alone. Don't sing out your information all over the place."

"You're going straight ahead with your investigations, then?" Bannard asked of the detective.

"Yes, but we can't do much till after the funeral, and——"

"And what?"

"And after the reading of the will. You know motive is a strong factor in unraveling a murder case. Why, s'pose some of the servants receive large legacies; and you know how queer Mrs. Pell was—she might well leave a fortune to those Purdys."

"Oh, they didn't do it," and Bannard tossed off the idea as absurd.

"You don't know. Leaving out, as I said before, the question of how the villain got in or out, it might easily have been one or more of the servants. And other help is hired beside the regular house crowd. Take it from me, it was somebody in the house, and not an intruder from outside."

"And take it from me, you don't know what you're talking about," said Roger Downing, as he angrily stalked away.

Bannard had said very little to Iris since his coming to Pellbrook, but he now sought her out, and asked her what she thought about the whole matter.

"I don't know what to think," Iris replied to his question, "but I don't know as it matters so much about solving the mystery. Poor Aunt Ursula is dead, she was killed, but I don't see how we can find out who did it. I think, Win, it must have been somebody we don't know about—say, someone connected with her early life—you know, she has had a more or less varied career."

"How do you mean? She lived here very quietly."

"Yes, but before she came here. Before we knew her, even before we were born. And then, her jewels. Nobody ever owned a splendid collection of jewels but what they were beset by robbers and burglars to get the treasure."

"Then you think it an ordinary jewel robbery?"

"Not ordinary! Far from that! But I can't help thinking that was what the thieves were after. Why, you know her jewels are world famous."

"What do you mean by world famous?"

"Well, maybe not that, but well known among jewelers and jewel collectors. So they would, of course, be known to professional jewel thieves."

"That's so. Where are they anyway?"

"The thieves?"

"No; the jewels."

"I haven't the least idea——"

"Haven't you? Honestly!"

"Indeed, I haven't."

"I don't believe you."

"Why, Win Bannard, what do you mean!"

"Oh, I oughtn't to say that, but truly, Iris, I supposed of course you knew where Aunt Ursula kept 'em."

"Well, I don't. I've not the slightest notion of her hiding place."

"Hiding place! Aren't they in a safe deposit, or something of that sort?"

"They may be, but I don't think so. But it will be told in the will. Mr. Chapin is so ridiculously secretive about the will! Sometimes I think she may have left them all to someone else after all."

"Someone else?"

"Yes, someone besides us. I think, don't you, that we ought to be her principal heirs? But she promised me, always, her wonderful diamond pin."

"Huh! I don't think one diamond pin so much! Why, she has——"

"I know, but she always spoke of this particular diamond pin that she destined for me as something especially valuable. I expect it is a sort of Kohinoor."

"Oh, I didn't know about that. And what is she going to leave me, to match up to that?"

"I don't know, I'm sure. But we sound very mercenary, talking like this, before the poor lady is even buried."

"To be honest, Iris, I'm terribly sorry for the way the poor thing was killed, but I can't grieve very deeply, unless I'm a hypocrite. As you know, Aunt Ursula and I weren't good friends——"

"Who could be friends with Aunt Ursula? I tried my best, Win, my very best, but she was too trying to live with! You've no idea what I went through!"

"Oh, yes, I've an idea. I lived with her some years myself. Well, we'll say nothing but good of her now she's gone. I say, Iris, let's take a walk down to the village and see Browne, the jeweler."

"What for?"

"Ask him about her jewels."

"Oh, no, I think that would be horrid. You go, if you like. I shan't."

But Iris went out on the verandah with Bannard, and they ran into Sam Torrey, the brother of Agnes.

"Hello, Sam," said Bannard. "What's that you were saying about seeing a man around here Sunday morning."

"Not morning, but noon," declared Sam, gazing with lack-luster eyes at his questioner.

"Brace up, now, Sam, tell me all you know," and Bannard looked the boy squarely in the eye.

Sam, about seventeen, or so, was of undeveloped intellect, called by the neighbors half-witted. But if pinned down to a subject and his attention kept on it, he could talk pretty nearly rationally.

"Know lots. Saw man here—there—near edge of woods—nice little car, oh, awful nice little car——"

"Yes, go on, what did he do?"

"Do? Do? Oh, nothing. Walked around——"

"Hold on, you said he was in a car."

"No, walked around, sly—oh, so sly——"

"Rubbish! you're making up!"

"Of course he is," said Iris, "he can't tell a connected story. Who was the man, Sam?"

"Don't know name. But—he was at the show to-day."

"At the inquest! No!" Bannard exclaimed.

"Yes, he was. Same man. Oh, I know him, he killed Missy Pell."

"How did he get in the house," Bannard tried to draw him on to further absurd assertions.

"Dunno," and Sam shook his uncertain head. "But he did, and he kill—and kill—and so, he come to show."

"Fool talk!" and Bannard scowled at the defective lad.

"No, sir! Sam no fool."

"Yes, you are, and you know it," Iris declared, but she smiled at him, for she had known the unfortunate boy a long time, and always treated him kindly, but not as a rational human being.

And just then, Browne, the local jeweler, appeared.

He had been sent for by Hughes, in order that they might get some idea of the whereabouts of Mrs. Pell's jewel collection. No one really thought they had all been stored in the small wall safe, and Browne was asked concerning his knowledge.

Several of those most interested clustered round to hear the word and perhaps none was more eager than Mr. Bowen. Quite evidently he had strong hopes of receiving the chalice for his church, and he listened to the jeweler's story.

But it was of little value. Mr. Browne declared his knowledge of many of Mrs. Pell's jewels, which she had shown him, asking his opinion or merely to gratify his interest, and again, when she had wanted to sell some of the smaller ones. But he was sure that she possessed many and valuable stones that he had never seen. He named some diamonds and emeralds that were of sufficient size and weight to be designated by name. He told of some collections that she had bought with his knowledge and advice. And he assured them that he was positive she was the owner of at least two million dollars' worth of unset gems, part of which formed the collection left to her by her husband and part of which she had acquired later, herself.

But Mr. Browne hadn't the slightest idea where these gems were stored for safe keeping. He had sometimes discreetly hinted to Mrs. Pell that he would like to know where they were, merely as a matter of interest, but she had never told him, and had only stated that they were safe from fire, flood or thieves!

"Those were her very words," he asserted, "and when I said that was an all-round statement, she laughed and said they were buried."

"Buried!" cried Iris, "what an idea!"

"A very good idea," Mr. Browne defended. "I'm not sure that isn't the best way to conceal such a stock of valuables."

"But buried where?" pursued the girl.

"That I don't know," said the jeweler.

CHAPTER 6: LUCILLE

"I am Miss Lucille Darrel."

People are usually cognizant of their own names, but few could throw more convincing certainty into the announcement than the speaker. One felt sure at once that her name was as she stated and had been so for a long time. The first adjective one would think of applying to Miss Darrel would be "positive." She was that by every implication of her being. Her hair was positively white, her eyes positively black. Her manner and expression were positive, and her very walk, as she stepped into the Pellbrook living room, was positive and unhesitating.

Iris chanced to be there alone, for the moment; alone, that is, save for the casket containing the body of Ursula Pell. The great room, set in order for the funeral, was filled with rows of folding chairs, and the oppressive odor of massed flowers permeated the place.

The girl stood beside the casket, tears rolling down her cheeks and her whole body shaking with suppressed sobs.

"Why, you poor child," said the newcomer, in most heartfelt sympathy; "Are you Iris?"

The acquiescent reply was lost, as Miss Darrel gathered the slim young figure into her embrace. "There, there," she soothed, "cry all you want to. Poor little girl." She gently smoothed Iris' hair, and together they stood, looking down at the quiet, white face.

"You loved her so," and Miss Darrel's tone was soft and kind.

"I did," Iris said, feeling at once that she had found a friend. "Oh, Miss Darrel, how kind you are! People think I didn't love Aunt Ursula, because—because we were both high-tempered, and we did quarrel. But, underneath, we were truly fond of each other, and if I seem cold and uncaring, it isn't the truth; it's because—because——"

"Never mind, dear, you may have many reasons to conceal your feelings. I know you loved her, I know you revere her memory, for I saw you as I entered, when you thought you were all alone——"

"I am alone, Miss Darrel—I am very lonely. I'm glad you have come, I've been wanting to see you. It's all so terrible—so mysterious; and—and they suspect me!"

Iris' dark eyes stared with fear into the kind ones that met hers, and again she began to tremble.

"Now, now, my child, don't talk like that. I'm here, and I'll look after you. Suspect you, indeed! What nonsense. But it's most inexplicable, isn't it? I know so little, only what I've read in the papers. I came from Albany last night; I started as soon as I possibly could, and traveled as fast as I could. I want to hear all about it, but not from you. You're worn out, you poor dear. You ought to be in bed this minute."

"Oh, no, Miss Darrel, I'm all right. Only—I've a lot on my mind, you see, and—and——" again Iris, with a glance of distress at the cold, dead face, burst into tumultuous weeping.

"Come out of this room," said Miss Darrel, positively. "It only shakes your nerves to stay here. Come, show me to my room. Where shall I lodge? This house is mine, now, or soon will be. You knew that, didn't you?"

"Yes," said Iris, listlessly. "I knew Aunt Ursula meant to leave it to you, but I don't know whether she did or not. And I don't care. I only care for one thing——"

But Miss Darrel was not listening. She was observing and admiring the house itself—the colonial staircase, the well-proportioned rooms and halls, and the attractive furnishings.

"I'll give you the rose guest room," Iris said, leading her toward it, as they reached the upper hall. "Winston Bannard is here, but no other visitors. If there are other heirs, I suppose Mr. Chapin has notified them."

"I suppose so," returned Miss Darrel, preoccupiedly. "When will the services be held?"

"This afternoon at two. It will be a large funeral. Everybody in Berrien knew Aunt Ursula, and people will come up from New York. Now, have you everything you want to make you comfortable in here?"

"Yes, thank you," replied Miss Darrel, after a quick, comprehensive glance round the room, "and, wait a moment, Iris—mayn't I call you Iris?"

"Yes, indeed, I'm glad to have you."

"I only want to say that I want to be your friend. Please let me and come to me freely for comfort or advice or anything I can do to help you."

"Thank you, Miss Darrel, I am indeed glad to have a friend, for I am lonely and frightened. But I can't say more now, someone is calling me."

Iris ran downstairs and found Winston Bannard eagerly asking for her.

"I've unearthed Aunt Ursula's diary!" he exclaimed.

"Was it hidden?"

"Not exactly, but old Hughes wouldn't let me rummage around in the desk much, so I took a chance when he was out of the way, and it was in an upper drawer. Come on, let's go and read it."

"Why? Now?"

"Yes. Look here, Iris, you want to trust me in this thing. You want to let me take care of you."

"Thank you, Win—I'm glad to have you——" but Iris spoke constrainedly, "By the way, Miss Darrel is here."

"Who's she? Oh, that cousin of Aunt Ursula's?"

"Not really her cousin, but a relative of Mr. Pell's. I never knew her, did you?"

"No; what's she like?"

"Oh, she's lovely. Kind and capable, but rather dictatorial, or, at least, decided."

"Does she get the house?"

"She says so. And I know Auntie spoke of leaving it to her, because, I believe, Mr. Pell had wished it."

"What about the jewels, Iris?"

"Oh, Win, I wish you wouldn't talk or think about those things, till after——"

"After the funeral? I know it seems strange—I know I seem mercenary, and all that, but it isn't so, Iris. There's something wrong going on, and unless we are careful and alert, we'll lose our inheritance yet."

"What *do* you mean?"

"Never mind. But come with me and let's take a glimpse into the diary. I tell you we ought to do it. It may mean everything."

Iris followed him to a small enclosed porch off the dining room and they put their heads together over the book.

It was funny, for Ursula Pell couldn't help being funny.

One entry read:

"Felt like the old scratch to-day, so took it out on Iris. Poor girl, I am ashamed of myself to tease her so, but she's such a good-natured little ninny, she stands it as few girls would. I must make it up to her in some way."

And another read at random:

"Up a stump to-day for some mischief to get into. Satan doesn't look out properly for my idle hands. I manicured them carefully, and sat waiting for some real nice mischief to come along, but none did, so I hunted up some for myself. It's Agnes' night out, and I stuffed the kitchen door keyhole with putty. Won't she be mad! She'll have to ring Polly up, and she'll be mad, too. I'll give Agnes my black lace parasol, to make up. What a scamp I am! I feel like little Toddie, in 'Helen's Babies,' who used to pray, 'Dee Lord, not make me sho bad!' Well, I s'pose 'tis my nature to."

"These are late dates," said Bannard, running over the leaves, "let's look further back."

It was not a yearly diary, but a goodsized blank book, in which the writer had jotted down her notes as she felt inclined; something was written every day, but it might be a short paragraph or several pages in length.

"Here's something about us," and Bannard pointed to a page:

The entry ran:

"To-day I gave the box for Iris into Mr. Chapin's keeping. I shall never see it again. After I am gone, he will give it to I. and she can have it for what it is worth. I'll leave the F. pocket-book to Winston. The house must go to Lucille, but the young people won't mind that, as they will have enough."

"That's all right, isn't it, Iris. Looks as if we were the principal heirs."

"You can't tell, Win. She may have changed her mind a dozen times."

"That's so. Let's see if there's anything about Mr. Bowen and his chalice."

"Oh, she only thought of that last Sunday."

"Don't be too sure. I shouldn't be surprised if the old chap got round her long ago, and had the matter all fixed up, and she pretended it was a new idea."

"I can't think that."

"You can't, eh? Well, listen here:

"'Sometimes I think it would be a good deed to use half of the jewels for a gift to the church. If I should take the whole Anderson lot, there would be plenty left for W. and I.'"

"What is the Anderson lot?" Iris asked.

"A certain purchase that the old man got through a dealer or an agent, named Anderson. Aunt Ursula used to talk over these things with me and, all of a sudden she shut up on the subject and never mentioned jewels to me again."

"She talked of them to me, sometimes, but never anything of definite importance. She spoke of the Baltimore emeralds, but I know nothing of them."

"They're mentioned here; see:

"'The Balto. emeralds will make a wonderful necklace for I. when she gets older. I hope I may live long enough to see the child decked out in them. I believe I'll tell her the jewels are all in the crypt.'"

"In the crypt! Oh, Win, you know Mr. Browne said he thought they were buried! Isn't a crypt a burial place in a church?"

"Yes; but a crypt may be anywhere. Any vault is a crypt, really."

"But a bank vault wouldn't be called a crypt, would it?"

"Not generally speaking, no. But, she probably changed the hiding place a dozen times since this was written."

"Well, we'll know all when we hear the will. Isn't it a queer thing to put all of one's fortune in jewels?"

"She didn't do it, her husband did. And everybody says he was a shrewd old chap. And, you know he made wonderful collections of coins and curios, and all sorts of things."

"Yes, up in the attic is a big portfolio of steel engravings. I can't admire them much, but they're valuable, Auntie said once. It seems Uncle Pell was a perfect crank on engravings of all sorts."

"I know. She gave me an intaglio topaz for a watch-fob. I didn't care much about it."

"I'm crazy to see my diamond pin. I've heard about that for years. No matter how often she changed her will, she told me, that diamond pin was always bequeathed to me. Perhaps it's her choicest gem."

"Perhaps. Listen to this, Iris:

"'I am going to New York next Tues. I shall give Winston a cheap-looking pair of gloves, but I shall first put a hundred-dollar bill in each finger.'

"She did that, you know, and I was so mad when she gave them to me I was within an ace of throwing them away. But I caught sight of a bulge in the thumb, and I just thought, in time, there might be some joke on. Didn't she beat the dickens?"

"She did. Oh, Win, you don't know how she humiliated and hurt me! But I'm sorry, now, that I wasn't more patient."

"You were, Iris! Here's proof!

"'I put a wee little toad in Iris' handbag to-day. We were going to the village, and when she opened the bag, Mr. Toad jumped out! Iris loathes toads, but I must say she took it beautifully. I bought her a muff and stole of Hud. seal to make up.'"

"Poor auntie," said Iris, as the tears came, "she always wanted to 'make up!' I believe she couldn't help those silly tricks, Win. It was a sort of mania with her."

"Pshaw! She could have helped it if she'd wanted to. Somebody's coming, put the book away now."

The somebody proved to be Miss Darrel, who, when Bannard was presented, gave him a cordial smile, and proceeded to make friendly advances at once.

"We three are the only relatives present," she said, "and we must sympathize with and help one another."

"You can help me," said Iris, who was irresistibly drawn to the strong, efficient personality, "but I fear I can't help you. Though I am more than willing."

"It is a pleasure just to look at you, my dear, you are so sweet and unspoiled."

Bannard gave Miss Darrel a quick glance. Her speech, to him, savored of sycophancy.

But not to Iris. She slipped her hand into that of her new friend, and gave her a smile of glad affection.

Luncheon was announced and after that came the solemn observances of the funeral.

As Miss Darrel had said, the three were the only relatives present. Ursula Pell had other kin, but none were nearby enough to attend the funeral. Of casual friends there were plenty, and of neighbors and villagers enough to fill the house, and more too.

Iris heard nothing of the services. Entirely unnerved, she lay on the bed in her own room, and sobbed, almost hysterically.

Agnes brought sal volatile and aromatic ammonia, but the sight of the maid roused Iris' excitement to a higher pitch, and finally Miss Darrel took complete charge of the nervous girl.

"I'm ashamed of myself," Iris said, when at last she grew calmer, "but I can't help it. There's a curse on the house—on the place—on the family! Miss Darrel, save me—save me from what is about to befall!"

"Yes, dear, yes; rest quietly, no harm shall come to you. The shock has completely upset you. You've borne up so bravely, and now the reaction has come and you're feverish and ill. Take this, my child, and try to rest quietly."

Iris took the soothing draught, and fell, for a few moments, into a troubled slumber. But almost immediately she roused herself and sat bolt upright.

"I didn't kill her!" she said, her large dark eyes burning into Miss Darrel's own.

"No, no, dear, you didn't kill her. Never mind that now. We'll find it all out in good time."

"I don't want it found out! It must not be found out! Won't you take away that detective man? He knows too much—oh, yes, he knows too much!"

"Hush, dear, please don't make any disturbance now. They're taking your aunt away."

"Are they?" and suddenly Iris calmed herself, and stood up, quite still and composed. "Let me see," she said; "no, I don't want to go down. I want to look out of the windows."

Kneeling at the front window of Miss Darrel's room, in utter silence, Iris watched the bearers take the casket out of the door.

"Poor Aunt Ursula," she whispered softly, "I *did* love you. I'm sorry I didn't show it more, I wish I had been less impatient. But I will avenge your death. I didn't think I could, but I must—I know I *must*, and I will do it. I promise you, Aunt Ursula—I vow it!"

"Who killed her?" Miss Darrel spoke softly, and in an awed tone.

"I can't tell you. But I—*I* am the avenger!"

It was an hour or more later when the group gathered in the living room, listened to the reading of Ursula Pell's last will and testament.

Mr. Bowen's round face was solemn and sad. Mrs. Bowen was pale with weeping.

Miss Darrel kept a watchful eye on Iris, but the girl was quite her normal self. Winston Bannard was composed and somewhat stern looking, and the servants huddled in the doorway waiting their word.

As might have been expected from the eccentric old lady, the will was long and couched in a mass of unnecessary verbiage. But it was duly drawn and witnessed and its decrees were altogether valid.

As was anticipated, the house and estate of Pellbrook were bequeathed to Miss Lucille Darrel.

The positive nod of that lady's head expressed her satisfaction, and Mr. Chapin proceeded.

Followed a few legacies of money or valuables to several more distant relatives and friends, and then came the list of servants.

A beautiful set of cameos was given to Agnes; a collection of rare coins to the Purdys; and a wonderful gold watch with a jeweled fob to Campbell.

A clause of the will directed that, "if any of the legatees prefer cash to sentiment, they are entirely at liberty to sell their gifts, and it is recommended that Mr. Browne will make for them the most desirable agent.

"The greater part of my earthly possessions," the will continued, "is in the form of precious stones. These gems are safely put away, and their whereabouts will doubtless be disclosed in due time. The entire collection is together, in one place, and it is to be shared alike by my two nearest and dearest of kin, Iris Clyde and Winston

Bannard. And I trust that, in the possession and enjoyment of this wealth, they will forgive and forget any silly tricks their foolish old aunt may have played upon them.

"Also, I give and bequeath to my niece, Iris Clyde, the box tied with a blue silk thread, now in the possession of Charles Chapin. This box contains the special legacy which I have frequently told her should be hers.

"Also, I give and bequeath to my husband's nephew, Winston Bannard, the Florentine pocket-book, which is in the upper right-hand compartment of the desk in my sitting room, and which contains a receipt from Craig, Marsden & Co., of Chicago. This receipt he will find of interest."

"That pocket-book!" cried Bannard. "Why, that's the one the thief emptied!"

Everyone looked up aghast. The empty pocket-book, found flung on the floor of the ransacked room, was certainly of Florentine illuminated leather. But whether it was the one meant in the will, who knew?

After concluding the reading of the will, Mr. Chapin handed to Iris the box that had been intrusted to his care. It was very carefully sealed and tied with a blue silk thread.

Slowly, almost reverently, Iris broke the seals and opened the box. From it she took the covering bit of crumpled white tissue paper, and found beneath it a silver ten-cent piece and a common pin.

"A dime and pin!" cried Bannard instantly; "one of Aunt Ursula's jokes! Well, if that isn't the limit!"

Iris was white with indignation. "I might have known," she said, "I might have known!"

With an angry gesture she threw the dime far out of the window, and cast the pin away, letting it fall where it would.

CHAPTER 7: THE CASE AGAINST BANNARD

"It's just this way," said Lucille Darrel, positively, "this house is mine, and I want it to myself. Ursula Pell is dead and buried and she can't play any more tricks on anybody. I admit that was a hard joke on you, Iris, to get a dime and pin, when for years you've been expecting a diamond pin! I can't help laughing every time I think of it! But all the same, that's your business, not mine. And, of course, you and Mr. Bannard will get your jewels yet, somehow. That woman left some explanation or directions how to find her hoard of gems. You needn't tell me she didn't."

"That's just it, Miss Darrel," and Iris looked deeply perplexed, "I've never known Aunt Ursula to play one of her foolish tricks but what she 'made it up' as she called it, to her victim. Why, her diary is full of planned jokes and played jokes, but always it records the amends she made. I think yet, that somewhere in that diary we'll find the record of where her jewels are."

"I don't," declared Bannard. "I've read the thing through twice; and it does seem to have vague hints, but nothing of real importance."

"I've read it too, at least some of it," and Miss Darrel looked thoughtful, "and I think the reference to the crypt is of importance. Also, I think her idea of having a jeweled chalice made is in keeping with the idea of a crypt as a hiding-place. What more like Ursula Pell than to manage to hide her gems in the crypt of a church and then desire to leave a chalice to that church."

"There's no crypt in the Episcopal church here," objected Iris.

"I didn't say here. The church, I take it, is in some other place. She had no notion of giving a chalice to Mr.

Bowen, she just teased him about that, but she meant it
for some church in Chicago, where she used to live, or up
in that little Maine town where she was brought up and
where her father was a minister."

"This may all be so," Bannard admitted, "but it's pure
supposition on your part."

"Have you any better supposition? Any other theory?
Any clear direction in which to look?"

"No;" and the young man frowned; "I haven't. I think
that dime and pin business unspeakably small and mean!
I put up with those tricks as long as I could stand them,
but to have them pursue me after Mrs. Pell is dead is a
little too much! It's none of it *her* family's fortune,
anyway. My uncle, Mr. Pell, owned the jewels and left
them to her. She did quite right in dividing them between
her own niece and myself, but far from right in so
secreting them that they can't be found. And they never
will be found! Of that I'm certain. The will itself said they
would *doubtless* be discovered! What a way to put it!"

"That's all so, Win," Iris spoke wearily, "but we must
try to find them. Couldn't that crypt be in this house, not
in any church?"

Bannard looked at the girl curiously. "Do you think
so?" he said, briefly.

"You mean a concealed place, I suppose," put in Miss
Darrel. "Well, remember this house is mine, now, and I
don't want any digging into its foundations
promiscuously. If you can prove to me by some good
architect's investigation that there is such a place or any
chance of such a place, you may open it up. But I won't
have the foundations undermined and the cellars dug
into, hunting for a crypt that isn't there!"

"Of course we can't prove it's here until we find it, or
find some indications of it," Iris agreed. "But you've
invited us both to stay here for a week or two——"

"I know I did, but I wish I hadn't, if you're going to
tear down my house——"

"Now, now, Miss Darrel," Bannard couldn't help laughing at her angry face, "we're not going to pull the house down about your ears! And if you don't want Iris and me to visit you, as you asked us to, just say so and we'll mighty soon make ourselves scarce! We'll go to the village inn to-day, if you like."

"No, no; don't be so hasty. Take a week, Iris, to get your things together, and you stay that long, too, Mr. Bannard; but, of course, it isn't strange that I should want my house to myself after a time."

"Not at all, Miss Lucille," Iris smiled pleasantly, "you are quite justified. I will stay a few days, and then I shall go to New York and live with a girl friend of mine, who will be very glad to have me."

"And I will remain but a day or two here," said Bannard, "and though I may be back and forth a few times, I'll stay mostly in my New York rooms. I admit I rather want to look around here, for it seems to me that, as heirs to a large fortune of jewels, it's up to Iris and myself to look first in the most likely hiding-places for them; and where more probable than the testator's own house? Also, Miss Darrel, there will yet be much investigation here, in an endeavor to find the murderer; you will have to submit to that."

"Of course, I shall put no obstacles in the way of the law. That detective Hughes is a most determined man. He said yesterday, just before the funeral, that to-day he should begin his real investigations."

And the detective made good his promise. He arrived at Pellbrook and announced his determination to make a thorough search of the place, house and grounds.

"That crypt business," he declared, for he had read the diary, "means a whole lot. It's no church vault, my way of thinking, it's a crypt in this here house and the jewels are there. Mark that. Also, the concealed crypt is part of or connected with the secret passage that leads into that room, where the windows are barred, and that's how the murderer got in—or, at least, how he got out."

"But—but there isn't any such crypt," and Iris looked at him imploringly. "If there were, don't you suppose I'd know it?"

"You might, and then, again, you mightn't," returned Hughes; then he added, "and then again, mebbe you do."

A painful silence followed, for the detective's tone and glance, even more than his words, hinted an implication.

"And I wish you'd tell me," he went on, to Iris, "just what that funny business about the ten cent piece means. Did your aunt tell you she was going to leave you a real diamond?"

"Yes; for years Mrs. Pell has repeatedly told me that in her will she had directed that I was to receive a small box from her lawyer, which contained a diamond pin. That is, I thought she said a diamond pin; but of course I know now that she really said, 'a dime and pin.' That is not at all surprising, for it was the delight of her life to tease people in some such way."

"But she knew you *thought* she meant a diamond pin?"

"Of course, she did."

"She never put it in writing?"

"No; then she would have had to spell it, and spoil the joke. I don't resent that little trick, it was part of her nature to do those things."

"Did she never refer to its value?"

"Not definitely. She sometimes spoke of the valuable pin that would some day be mine, or the important legacy I should receive, or the great treasure she had bequeathed to me, but I never remember of hearing her say it was a costly gem or a valuable stone. She was always particular to tell the literal truth, while intentionally misleading her hearer. You see I am so familiar with her jests that I know all these details. It seems to me, now, that I ought to have realized from the way she said 'dime an' pin' that she was tricking me. But few people pronounce *diamond* with punctilious care; nearly everybody says 'di'mond'."

"Not in New England," observed Lucille Darrel, positively.

"Perhaps not," agreed Iris. "But anyway, it never occurred to me that she meant anything else than a diamond pin, and one of her finest diamonds at that. However, as I said, it isn't that joke of hers that troubles me, so much as the thought that she left her entire collection of jewels to Mr. Bannard and myself and gave us no instructions where to find them. It isn't like her to do that. Either she has left directions, which we must find, or she fully intended to do so, and her sudden death prevented it. That's what I'm afraid of. She was of rather a procrastinating nature, and also, greatly given to changing her mind. Now, she distinctly states in her diary that the jewels are all in the crypt, and I am firmly convinced that she intended to, or did, tell where that crypt is. If we can't find any letter or other revelation, we must look for the crypt itself, but I confess I think that would be hunting a needle in a haystack; for Aunt Ursula had a varied life, and before she settled down here she lived in a dozen different cities in many parts of the world."

"You're right, Miss Clyde," and Hughes nodded, "she prob'ly left some paper telling where that crypt is situated. Me, I believe it's in this house, but all the same, we've got to look mighty sharp. I don't want to miss it, I can tell you. Sorry, Miss Darrel, but we'll have to go through your cellar with a keen search."

"That's all right," Miss Darrel acquiesced. "I'm more than willing to allow a police hunt, but I don't want every Tom, Dick and Harry pulling my house to pieces."

"Lucky my name's Winston," said Bannard, good-naturedly. "Do you mind if I go with the strong arm of the law?"

"No," said his hostess, "and don't misunderstand me, young man. I've nothing against you, personally, but I don't admit your rights, as I do those of the police."

"I know; I understand," and Bannard followed the detective down the cellar stairs.

All this occurred the day after Ursula Pell's funeral. In the four days that had elapsed since her inexplicable death, no progress had been made toward solving the mystery. The coroner's inquest had brought out no important evidence, there were no clues that promised help, and though the police were determined and energetic, they had so little to work on that it was discouraging.

But Hughes was a man of bull-dog grit and perseverance. He argued that a mysterious murder had been committed and the mystery had to be solved and the murderer punished. That was all there was about it. So, to work. And his work began, in accordance with the dictates of his judgment, in the cellar of Ursula Pell's house.

And it ended there, for that day. No amount of scrutiny, of sounding walls or measuring dimensions brought forth the slightest suspicion, hope, or even possibility of a secret vault or crypt within the four walls. Hughes had two assistants, skilled builders both. Bannard added his efforts, but no stone or board was there that hadn't its own honest use and place.

Coal bins, ash pits, wood boxes, cupboards and portable receptacles were investigated with meticulous care, and the result was absolutely nothing to bear out the theory of a crypt of any sort or size, concealed or otherwise.

"And that settles that notion," summed up Hughes, as he made his report to the two interested women. "Of course, you must see, there's two ways to approach this case—one being from the question of how the murderer got in and out of that room, and the other being who the murderer was. Of course, if we find out either of those things, we're a heap forrader toward finding out the other. See?"

"I see," said Miss Darrel, "but I should think you'd find it easier to work on your first question. For here's the room, the door, the lock, and all those things. But as to the murderer, he's gone!"

"Clearly put, ma'am! And quite true. But the room and lock—in plain sight though they are—don't seem to be of any help. Whereas, the murderer, though he's gone, may not be able to stay gone."

"Just what do you mean by that?" asked Bannard.

"Two things, sir. One is, that they do say a murderer always returns to the scene of his crime."

"Rubbish! I've heard that before! It doesn't mean a thing, any more than the old saw that 'murder will out' is true."

"All right, sir, that's one; then, again, there's a chance that said murderer may not be able to stay away because we may catch him."

"That's the talk!" said Bannard. "Now you've said something worth while. Get your man, and then find out from him how he accomplished the impossible. Or, rather, the seemingly impossible. For, since somebody did enter that room, there was a way to enter it."

"It isn't the entering, you know, Mr. Bannard. Everybody was out of the living room at the time, and the intruder could have walked right in the side door of that room, and through into Mrs. Pell's sitting room. The question is, how did he get out, after ransacking the room and killing the lady, and yet leave the door locked after him."

"All right, that's your problem then. But, as I said, if he *did* do it, or *since* he did do it, somebody ought to be able to find out how."

"I'll subscribe to that, somebody *ought* to be able to, but who is the somebody?"

"Don't ask me, I'm no detective."

"No, sir. Now, Mr. Bannard, what about this? Do you think that Florentine pocket-book, that was found emptied, as if by the robber, is the one that your aunt left you in her will?"

"I think it is, Mr. Hughes. But I am by no means certain. Indeed, I suppose it, only because it looks as if it had held something of value which the intruder cared enough for to carry off with him."

"You think it looks that way?"

"I don't," interposed Iris. "I think there was nothing in it, and that's why it was flung down. If it had had contents the thief would have taken pocket-book and all."

"Not necessarily," said Bannard. "But it's all supposition. If that's the pocket-book my aunt willed to me, it's worthless now. If there is another Florentine pocket-book, I hope I can find it. You see, Miss Darrel, we'll have to make a search of my aunt's belongings. Why all the jewels may be hidden in among her clothing."

"No," and Iris shook her head decidedly. "Aunt Ursula never would have done that."

"Oh, I don't think so, either, but we *must* hunt up things. She may have had a dozen Florentine pocket-books, for all I know."

"But the will said, in the desk," Iris reminded him. "And there's no other in the desk, and that one has been there for a long time. I've often seen it there."

"You have?" said Hughes, a little surprised. "What was in it?"

"I never noticed. I never thought anything about it, any more than I thought of any other book or paper in Mrs. Pell's desk. She didn't keep money in it, that I know. But she did keep money in that little handbag, quite large sums, at times."

"Well," Hughes said, at last, by way of a general summing up, "I've searched the cellar, and I've long since searched the room where the lady died, and now I must ask permission to search the room above that one."

"Of course," agreed Miss Darrel. "That's your room, Iris."

"Yes; the detective is quite at liberty to go up there at once, so far as I am concerned."

The others remained below while Hughes and Iris went upstairs.

But after a few minutes they returned, and Hughes declared that all thought of any secret passage from Iris' room down to her aunt's sitting room was absolutely out of the question.

"This house is built about as complicatedly as a packing-box!" he laughed. "There's no cubby or corner unaccounted for. There are no thickened walls or unexplained bulges, or measurements that don't gee. No, sir-ee! However that wretch got out of that locked room, it was not by means of a secret exit. I'll stake my reputation on that! Now, having for the moment dismissed the question of means or method from my mind, I want to ask a few questions of one concerning whom, I frankly admit, I am in doubt. Mr. Bannard, you've no objection, of course, to replying?"

"Of course not," returned Bannard, but he suddenly paled.

Iris, too, turned white, and caught her breath quickly. "Don't you answer, Win," she cried; "don't you say a word without counsel!"

"Why, Iris, nonsense! Mr. Hughes isn't—isn't accusing me——"

"I'll put the questions, and you can do as you like about answering." Hughes spoke a little more gruffly than he had been doing, and looked sternly at his man.

"Were you up in this locality on Sunday afternoon, Mr. Bannard?"

"I was not. I've told you so before."

"That doesn't make it true. How do you explain the fact that Mrs. Pell made out to you a check dated last Sunday?"

"I've already discussed that," Bannard spoke slowly and even hesitatingly, but he looked Hughes in the eye, and his glance didn't falter. "My aunt drew that check and sent it to me by mail——"

"We've proved she sent no letter to you on Sunday—"

"Oh, no, you haven't. You've only proved that Campbell didn't mail a letter from her to me."

Hughes paused, then went on slowly.

"All right, when did you get that letter?"

"How do you know I got it at all?"

"Because you've deposited the check in your bank in New York."

"And how did I deposit it?"

"By mail, from here, day before yesterday."

"Certainly I did. Well?"

But Bannard's jauntiness was forced. His voice shook and his fingers were nervously twisting.

Hughes continued sternly. "I ask you again, Mr. Bannard, how did you receive that check? How did it come into your possession?"

"Easily enough. I wrote to my hotel to forward my mail, and they did so. There were two or three checks, the one in question among them, and I endorsed them and sent them to the bank by mail. I frequently make my deposits that way."

"But, Mr. Bannard, I have been to your hotel; I have interviewed the clerk who attended to forwarding your mail, and he told me there was no letter from Berrien."

"He overlooked it. You can't expect him to be sure about such a minor detail."

"He was sure. If Mrs. Pell did mail you that check in a letter on Sunday, it would have reached New York on Monday. By that time the papers had published accounts of the mysterious tragedy up here, and any letter from this town would attract attention, especially one addressed to the nephew of the victim of the crime."

"That's what happened, however," and Bannard succeeded in forcing a smile. "If you don't believe it, the burden of proof rests with you."

"No, sir, we *don't* believe it. We believe that you were up here on Sunday, that you received that check from the lady's own hand, that the half-burned cigarette was left in that room by you, and the New York paper also. In addition to this, we believe that you abstracted the paper of value from the Florentine pocket-book, and that you were the means of Mrs. Pell's death, whether by actual murder, or by attacking her in a fit of anger and cruelly maltreating her, finally flinging her to the floor, with murderous intent! You were seen hanging around the nearby woods about noon, and concealed yourself somewhere in the house while the family were at dinner. These things are enough to warrant us in charging you with this crime, and you are under arrest."

A shrill whistle brought two men in from outside, and Winston Bannard was marched to jail.

CHAPTER 8: RODNEY POLLOCK APPEARS

The shock of Bannard's arrest caused the complete collapse of Iris. Miss Darrel put the girl to bed and sent for Doctor Littell. He prescribed only rest and quiet and ordinary care, saying that a nurse was unnecessary, as Iris' physical health was unaffected and he knew her well enough to feel sure that she would recuperate quickly.

And she did. A day or two later she was herself again, and ready to follow up her determination to avenge the death of Ursula Pell.

"It's too absurd to suspect Win!" she said to the Bowens, who called often. "That boy is no more guilty than I am! Of course, he wasn't up here last Sunday! But no one will believe in his innocence until the real murderer is found. And I'm going to find him, and find the jewels, and solve the whole mystery!"

"There, there, Iris," Miss Darrel said, soothingly, for she thought the girl still hysterical, "don't think about those things now."

"Not think about them!" cried Iris, "why, what else can I think of? I've thought of nothing else for the whole week. It's Saturday now, and in six days we've done nothing, positively nothing toward finding the criminal."

"Perhaps it would be better not to try," suggested Mr. Bowen, gently.

"You say that because you believe Win guilty!" Iris shot at him. "I *know* he wasn't! You don't think he was, do you, Mrs. Bowen?"

"I scarcely know what to think, Iris, it is all so mysterious. Even if Winston did commit the crime, how did he get out of the room?"

"That's a secondary consideration——"

"I don't think so," put in the rector. "I think that's the first thing to be decided. Knowing that one could speculate——"

Iris turned away wearily. Though fond of the gentle little Mrs. Bowen, she had never liked the pompous and self-important clergyman, and she rose now to greet someone who appeared at the outer door.

It was Roger Downing, who, always devoted to Iris, was now striving to earn her gratitude by showing his willingness to be of help in any way he might. He came every day, and though Iris was careful not to encourage him, she eagerly wanted to know just what he knew about Bannard's presence at Pellbrook on the day of the tragedy.

"It's this way," Downing expressed it. "Win was certainly up here last Sunday, for I saw him. Now, Iris, if you want me to say I was mistaken as to his identity, I'll say it—but, I wasn't."

"You mean, sir, you would tell an untruth?" said Mr. Bowen, severely.

"I mean just that," averred Downing; "I care far more for Miss Clyde and her wishes than I do for the Goddess of Truth. I'm sorry if I shock you, sir, but that is the fact."

Mr. Bowen indeed looked shocked, but Iris said, emphatically, "You *were* mistaken, Roger, you must have been!"

"Very well, then, I was," he returned, but everyone knew he was purposely making a misstatement.

"Where was he?" said Iris, altogether illogically.

"In the woods, near the orchard fence."

"Sunday afternoon?"

"No; not afternoon. I'm not just sure of the time, but it was about noon. I was taking a long walk; I'd been nearly to Felton Falls, and was coming home to dinner. I only caught a glimpse of him, and I didn't think anything about it, until—until he said he hadn't been out of New York city on Sunday."

"Then, if you only caught a glimpse," Iris said quickly, "it may easily have been someone else! And it doubtless was."

"Shall I say so? Or do you want the truth?"

Iris dropped her eyes and said nothing. But Mr. Bowen spoke severely; "Cease that nonsense, Roger. Tell what you saw, and tell it frankly. The truth must be told."

"It's better to tell it anyway," declared Lucille Darrel, "truth can't harm the innocent. But it seems to me Mr. Downing may be mistaken."

"No, I'm not mistaken. Why, he wore that gray suit with a Norfolk jacket, that I've seen him wear before this summer. And he had on a light gray tie, with a ruby stickpin. The sun happened to hit the stone and I saw it gleam. You know that pin, Iris?"

Iris knew it only too well, and she knew, moreover, that when Win came up Sunday evening he wore that same suit, and the same scarf and pin. He had gone back to town the next day for other clothing, but when he had rushed to Berrien in response to Iris' summons, he had not stopped to change.

And yet, she was not ready, quite, to believe Downing's story. Suppose, in enmity to Win, he had made this all up. He might easily describe clothing that he knew Winston possessed, without having seen him as he said he had.

Iris looked at Downing so earnestly that he quailed before her glance.

"I don't believe your story at all!" she said; "you are making it up, because you hate Win, and it's absurd on the face of it! If Win came up here on Sunday at noon, he would come in for dinner, of course——"

"Not if he came with sinister intent," interrupted Downing.

"I don't believe it! You have made up that whole yarn, and let me tell you, you didn't do it very cleverly, either! Why didn't you say you saw him in the afternoon? It would have been more convincing, and quite as true!"

"I wasn't near here myself in the afternoon. But I did pass here just before twelve, and I did see him." Downing's voice had a ring of truth. "However, after this, I shall say I did not see him. I know you prefer that I should."

He looked straight at Iris, and ignored Mr. Bowen's pained exclamation.

"Say whatever you like, it doesn't matter to me," the girl returned haughtily.

"It does matter to you—and to Win. So, I shall say I was mistaken and that I did not see Winston Bannard on Sunday. I shall expect you, Mr. Bowen, and you ladies, not to report this conversation to the police. If you are questioned concerning it, you must say what you choose. But you will not be questioned, unless someone now present tattles."

*   *   *   *   *

Later that day, Iris had another caller. He sent up no card, but Agnes told her that a Mr. Pollock wished to see her.

"Don't go down, if you don't want to," urged Lucille, "I'll see what he wants."

But Miss Darrel's presence was not satisfactory to the stranger. He insisted on seeing Miss Clyde.

So Iris came down to find a man of pleasant manner and correct demeanor, who greeted her with dignity.

"I ask but a few moments of your time, Miss Clyde. I am Rodney Pollock, home Chicago, business hardware, but as a recreation I am a collector."

"And you are interested in my late aunt's curios," suggested Iris. "I am sorry to disappoint you, but they are not available for sale yet, and, indeed, I doubt if they ever will be."

"Don't go too fast," Mr. Pollock smiled a little, "my collection is not of rare bibelots or valuable curios. Perhaps I'd better confide that I'm an eccentric. I gather things that, while of no real use to others, interest me. Now, what I want from you, and I am willing to pay a price for it, is the ten cent piece and the pin your aunt left to you in her will."

"What!" and Iris stared at him.

"I told you I was eccentric," he said, quietly, "more, I am a monomaniac, perhaps. But, also, I am a philosopher, and I know, that, as old Dr. Coates said, 'If you want to be happy, make a collection.' So I collect trifles, that, valueless in themselves, have a dramatic or historic interest; and I wish," he beamed with pride, "you could see my treasures! Why, I have a pencil that President Garfield carried in his pocket the day he was shot, and I have a shoelace that belonged to Charlie Ross, and——"

"What very strange things to collect!"

"Yes, they are. But they interest me. My business, hardware, is prosaic, and having an imaginative nature I let my fancy stray to these tragic mementoes of crime or disaster. I have a menu card from the Lusitania and a piece of queerly twisted glass from the Big Tom explosion. I look reverently upon the relics of sad disasters, and I value my collection as a numismatist his coins or an art collector his pictures."

"But it seems so absurd to ask for a common pin!"

"It may, but I would greatly like to have it. You see, it was an unusual gift. You didn't care for it, in fact, I have heard you indignantly spurned it."

"I did."

"They say, you expected a diamond pin, and your aunt left you a dime and pin! Is that so?"

"That is so."

"Pardon my smiling, but I think it's the funniest thing I ever heard. And I would greatly like to have that pin and that dime."

"I'm sorry to say it's impossible, as I flung them away, and I've no idea where they landed."

"If you had them would you sell them to me?"

"I'd give them to you, if I had them! Why, it was merely an ordinary dime, not an old or rare coin. And the pin was a common one."

"Yes, I know that, but the idea, you see, the strange bequest—oh, I greatly desire to have one or the other of those two things! Can't we find them? Where did you throw them?"

"The dime I remember throwing out of the window. It must have fallen in the grass, you never could find that! The pin, I tossed on the floor, I think——"

"Has the room been swept since?"

"No, it has not. It should have been, but we have been so upset in the house——"

"I quite understand. I have a home and family, and I know what housekeeping means. However, since the room has not been swept, may I look around a bit in it?"

"It is this room, the room we are in. I sat right here, when I opened the box. I threw the dime out of that window, and I flung the pin over that way. I confess to a quick temper, and I was decidedly indignant. Let us look for the pin, and if we find it you may have it."

Iris was pleasantly impressed by Mr. Pollock's manner and set him down in her mind as a ridiculous but good-natured lunatic—not really insane, of course, but a little hipped on the subject of mementoes.

At her permission, her visitor fell on hands and knees, and went quickly over the floor of the whole room. Iris with difficulty restrained her laughter at the nimble figure hopping about like a frog, and peering into corners and under the furniture.

She looked about also, but from the more dignified position of standing, or sitting on a chair or footstool.

The search grew interesting, and at last they considered it completed. Their joint result was four pins and a needle.

Mr. Pollock presented a chagrined face.

"It may be any one of these," he said, rucfully looking at the four pins.

"That's true," Iris agreed. "But you may have them all, if you wish."

"Can't you judge which it is? See, this one is extra large."

"Then that's not it. I know it was of ordinary size. I scarcely looked at it, but I know that. Nor was it this crooked one. It was straight, I'm sure. But it may easily have been either of these other two."

"Suppose I take these two, then, and put them in my collection, with the surety that one or other is the identical pin."

"Do so, if you like," and Iris gave him a humoring smile. "Now, do you care to hunt for the dime? If you do, there's the lawn. But I won't help you, the sun is too warm."

"I think I won't hunt, or if I do, it will be only a little. I have this pin, and that is sufficient for a memento of this case. I am on my way to a house in Vermont, where I hope to get a button that figured in a sensational tragedy up there. I thank you for being so kind and I would greatly prefer to pay you for this pin. I am not a poor man."

"Nonsense! I couldn't take money for a pin! You're more than welcome to it. And one of those two must be the one, for I'm sure there's no other pin on this floor."

"I'm sure of that, too. I looked most carefully. Good-by, Miss Clyde, and accept the gratitude of a man who has a foolish but innocent fad."

Iris bowed a farewell at the front door, and returned to the living-room smiling at the funny adventure.

Almost involuntarily she began to look over the floor again, searching for pins.

"Have you lost anything?" asked Agnes, coming by.

"No; I've been looking for a pin."

"Want one, Miss Iris? Here's one."

"No, I don't want a pin, I mean—I don't want—a pin." Iris concluded her sentence rather lamely, for she had been half inclined to tell Agnes the story of her visitor, when something restrained her.

Perhaps it was Agnes' expression, for the maid said, "Were you looking for the pin Mrs. Pell left you?"

"Yes, I was," said Iris, astonished at the query.

"I have it," Agnes went on. "I picked it up the day you threw it away."

"For gracious' sake! Why did you do that?"

"Because—that's a lucky pin. Miss Iris, your aunt had that pin for years."

"I know it; it's been years in that box Mr. Chapin held for me."

"But before that. When I first came to live with Mrs. Pell, she always wore a pin stuck in the front of her dress. Once I took it out, it looked so silly, you know. She blew me up terribly, and said if I ever disturbed her things again she'd discharge me. And I gave it back to her—I had stuck it in my own dress—and she wore it for a short time more, and then she didn't wear it. Even then, I wouldn't have thought anything much about it, but a maid who lived here before I did, said she lost a pin once that had been in the waist of Mrs. Pell's gown and they had an awful time about it."

"Did they find it?"

"I don't know. I think not. I think she took another pin for a 'Luck.' Why, Polly knew about it. She said when she heard what Mrs. Pell had left to you, that it might be the lucky pin."

"Oh, what foolishness! Well, Agnes, have you really got the pin that Aunt Ursula left to me?"

"Yes, ma'am, as soon as I saw you throw it away, I watched my chance to go and pick it up before Polly could get it."

"Do you want to keep it?"

"Not if you want it, Miss Iris. If not, I'd like to have it. I suppose it's superstitious, but it seems lucky to me."

"Go and get it, Agnes, and let me see it."

*   *   *   *   *

But the maid returned without the pin.

"I can't find it, Miss Iris. I put it on the under side of my own pincushion, and there's none there now. I asked Polly and she said she didn't touch it. Where could it have gone?"

"You used it unthinkingly. It doesn't matter, there's no such thing as a lucky pin, Agnes. You can just as well take any other pin out of Aunt Ursula's cushion—take one, if you like—and call that your 'Luck.' Don't be a silly!"

Iris smiled to think that neither of the pins her strange visitor carried off with him was the right one, after all. "But," she thought, "it makes no difference, anyway, as he thinks he has it. He's sure it's one of the two he has; if there were three uncertain ones it would be too complicated. Let the poor man rest satisfied. I wonder if he found the dime."

But looking from the window she could see no sign of her late caller, and she dismissed the subject from her mind at once.

*   *   *   *   *

Yet she had not heard the last of it.

In the evening mail a letter came for her. It was in an unfamiliar handwriting, and was written on a single plain sheet of paper.

The note ran:

MISS CLYDE,

DEAR MADAM:

I will pay you one hundred dollars for the pin left to you by your aunt. Please make every effort to find it, and lay it on the South gatepost to-night at ten o'clock. Don't let anybody see you. You will receive the money to-morrow by registered mail. No harm is meant, but I want to get ahead of that other man who is making a collection.

Put it in a box, and be sly about it. I'll get it all right. You don't know me, but I would scorn to write an anonymous letter, and I willingly sign my name,

WILLIAM ASHTON.

That evening Iris told Lucille all about it.

"What awful rubbish," commented that lady. "But I know people who make just such foolish collections. One friend of mine collects buttons from her friends' dresses. Why, I'm afraid to go there, with a gown trimmed with fancy buttons; she rips one off when you're not looking! It's really a mania with her. Now two men are after your pin. Have you got it? I'd sell it for a hundred dollars, if I were you. And that man will pay. Those collectors are generally honest."

"No; I haven't it." And Iris proceeded to tell of Agnes' connection with the matter.

"H'm, a Luck! I've heard of them, too. Sometimes they're worth keeping. Oh, no, I'm not really superstitious, but an old Luck is greatly to be reverenced, if nothing more. If that pin was Ursula's Luck, you ought to keep it, my dear."

"But I haven't it. If it is a Luck, and if its possession would help me—would help to free Win—I'd like to see the collector that could get it away from me!"

"Oh, it mightn't be so potent as all that, but after all, a Luck is a Luck, and I'd be careful how I let one get away."

"But it has got away. And, too, I let friend Pollock go off with the idea that he had it; now, if I were to let somebody else take it, Mr. Pollock would have good reason to chide me."

"But how did this other man know about it?"

"I've no idea, unless he and Pollock are friends and compare notes."

"But how did—what's his name?—Ashton, know it was lost?"

"That's so, how did he? It's very mysterious. What shall I do?"

"Nothing at all. You can't put it on the gatepost, if you don't know where it is. But I'd certainly try to find it. Ask Polly what she knows about it."

"I will, to-morrow. She's gone to bed by now. Poor old thing, she works pretty hard."

"I know it. I'll be glad when I get a whole staff of new servants. But I'll wait till this excitement is over."

That was Miss Darrel's attitude. She had received her inheritance and selfishly took little interest in that of the other heirs.

CHAPTER 9: IRIS IN DANGER

Wearily, Iris went upstairs to her own room, and closed the door. Then she opened it again, for the night was hot and stifling. Without turning on a light, she went and sat by an open window, leaning her arms on the sill, and staring, with unseeing gaze, out into the night.

She was thinking about Bannard, and her thoughts were in a chaos. Not for a moment did she believe him guilty of his aunt's death, but she could not help a conviction that he had been at Pellbrook that Sunday afternoon. She wasted no time on the inexplicable mystery of the locked room, for, she reasoned, whoever did kill Mrs. Pell escaped afterward, so that point had no bearing on Winston's connection with the crime. Moreover, she knew, as she feared the police also knew, that Bannard was deeply in debt, and as he had received the substantial check from his aunt, and had banked the same, it was all, in a way, circumstantial evidence that was strongly indicative.

Roger Downing had seen Win around Pellbrook about noon, or he thought he had, of that she was sure, and Roger's declaration that he would deny this was of little value, for Hughes would get it out of him, she knew.

Arrest wasn't conviction, to be sure, but—Iris resolutely put away her own growing suspicions of Bannard. She would stand by him, even in the face of evidence or testimony—she would—and then she began to speculate as to the fortune. Those gems were hidden somewhere—and without Winston to help her how was she to look for them? Knowing Ursula Pell's tricksy spirit, the jewels might be in the most absurd and unexpected place. Crypt? Where was any crypt? She inclined a little to the idea of its being in some church, not in Berrien; for with all Mrs. Pell's foolishness, Iris didn't think she would hide the treasure in any but a safe place. And too, the crypt might well be merely the vaults of some safe deposit company—in Chicago, perhaps, or New York. It was maddening! Iris thought over the events since the day of her aunt's death. The awful tragedy itself, the mystery of the unknown assailant and his manner of escape, the fearful scenes of the inquest, the funeral, and the police searchings since, and, finally, the arrest of Bannard. It seemed to Iris she couldn't stand anything more; and yet, she realized, it had but begun. The mystery was as deep as ever, the jewels were missing, perhaps would never be found, and Winston's case looked very dark against him.

"I *must* find the jewels," Iris mused, as she had done a hundred times before. "And I must do it by my wits. They are somewhere in safety—of that I'm sure, and, too, Aunt Ursula has left some hint, some clue to their hiding-place. If I'm to be of any help to Win, the first thing to do is to ferret out this matter. Then, we may be better able to trace the——"

Her thoughts were interrupted by the sight of what seemed to her to be a shadow, crossing the lawn below her. The shrubbery was dense, and the night dark, but she discerned a faint semblance of a person skulking among the trees. She sat motionless, but the shadow faded, and she could see nothing more of it. Concluding she had been mistaken, she sighed and was about to draw the blinds and make a light, when she was seized with a sudden spirit of nervous energy that impelled her to *do* something—anything, rather than go to bed, where she knew she would only toss sleeplessly on the pillow.

Silently, not to disturb Miss Darrel, she crossed the hall and went downstairs. With only a vague notion of looking around, she went into her aunt's sitting room, and flashed on a light. It was the table lamp that had been found broken on the floor at the time of the tragedy, but that now, replaced by a new electrolier, gave a pleasant, soft light. Coiling up the long green cord, lest she trip on it, Iris sank into an easy chair near the table.

Restlessly, she arose and walked about the room. Though familiar with every detail, it looked strange to her, as a room does when one is the sole occupant. She opened the wall-safe, and stared into its emptiness. She pulled open some drawers of a cabinet, looked into a few boxes, and with no definite purpose, sat down at her aunt's desk. Disinterestedly, she looked over some books and papers, but she knew them all by heart. She ran over some bundles of letters, hoping to find a penciled memorandum on the backs, that had been hitherto unnoticed.

Nothing met her eye that seemed important, and she turned from the desk, her glance falling on the cretonne window curtains that overhung the lighter lace ones.

"Come out!" she cried, and then quickly, "no, *don't* come out! Stay where you are! Who are you?"

The curtain moved very slightly, and Iris rose, and stood, holding the back of her chair. Her heart was beating wildly, for though possessed of average courage, to be alone at midnight in a room of sinister memories, and see the folds of a curtain sway ever so little is, to say the least, disturbing.

"Who are you, I say!" she repeated angrily, but there was no response, and the curtain hung still.

A terror passed through her, and left her shivering, with an icy grip at her heart. Though not at all inclined toward a belief in the supernatural, there was an uncanny feeling in the atmosphere and Iris trembled with a strange, weird feeling, as of impending disaster. She edged a step backward, but as she did so the curtain was flung aside, and a man stood disclosed—a tall figure, with strong, muscular frame, and arms extended in a threatening gesture.

"Not a word!" he whispered, "not a sound!" and the glint of a small revolver flashed toward her. But she was too petrified with fear to speak, for the man was masked, and the effect of the blackavised apparition took her breath away. Only for a moment, however, and then a wave of relief surged over her. For, alarming as a human intruder may be, he is less frightful than a supernatural visitant.

The color came back to her white cheeks, and she said scornfully, "I am not afraid of you——"

"You'd better be, then," and the man moved nearer to her. "I've no wish to harm you, but if you raise an alarm, I shall consider my own safety first!"

"Coward!"

"Nonsense! I don't mean before yours, you've nothing to fear. But if you're inclined to call help, I'll have to make it impossible for you to do so."

The voice was that of an educated man, but entirely unfamiliar to Iris. Her terror left her, as she realized that at least she hadn't to deal with a low-class, uncouth ruffian.

"Why should I call help, since you say I've nothing to fear?" she said, trying to speak coolly, but still watching the carefully held pistol.

"Nothing to fear if you do as I say."

"And what do you say?"

The masked figure came a little nearer. "I say——" he began, but Iris interrupted.

"Stay where you are! I am not afraid of your pistol; your voice tells me you would not shoot a defenceless woman, but I command you to keep your distance."

"My voice belies me, then," he returned coolly. "I'd shoot you quicker'n a wink, were it necessary to make my getaway. But, listen; you will be immediately unmolested, if you give me what I have come here to get. I advise you to give it willingly, but if not—then I must get it as best I can."

"Take off your mask, won't you?" and Iris' tone was almost formal. "I know you, don't I?"

"You do not, and something tells me you never will. Pardon me, if I retain my protecting decoration——"

"Scarcely a decoration," murmured Iris, who was striving to think quickly what to do.

"Thank you; that implies your belief in a fair share of good looks on my part. But that's a matter of no moment. And time passes. I am here to ask you for a matter of no great moment after all. I want the pin that your late aunt left you in her will."

"Oh, then you are William Ashton?"

"Careful! Not so loud. Yes—I am none other than he." A mock dramatic gesture accompanied the phrase, and Iris involuntarily smiled.

"You are charming when you smile," the visitor went on. "I may say that, since I am not making a social call——"

"You seem to be, I think," Iris interrupted him.

"Far from it! You are under a distinct misapprehension. But, alas! your smiles and charms are not the prize I'm seeking. I want that pin," for the first time he spoke a little roughly, "and I'm going to have it!"

"What under the heavens do you want of that pin?" exclaimed Iris, surprised beyond all thought of fear. She had at first supposed he was after the jewels, or money, at least.

"Never mind what for. Are you going to hand it over?"

"I suppose you are making a collection of dramatic trifles, like Mr. Pollock. It seems to be a popular pursuit, this gathering material for a miniature junk-shop!"

"So? Well, are you going to give it to me? Why didn't you put it on the gate post to-night?"

"For the very good reason that I haven't got it."

"Don't talk that useless chatter. Of course you have it."

"But I haven't. I threw it away, when the lawyer gave it to me, and——"

"No; you didn't. You only pretended to. Come; now, where is it?"

"Will you go away if I give it to you?" Iris was struck with an idea.

"If you give me your word of honor that you're giving me the right one."

This dissuaded her, for she had intended to give him one from her belt ribbon.

"I tell you I don't *know* where it is. Now, cease this useless interview, please, and leave me."

"I'll do nothing of the sort! You know where that pin is, and I am sure it's hidden in this room—"

"How utterly absurd you are! Why, *why* do you want it? I believe you're crazy!"

"I'm not, as you'll find out! But I intend to have the pin, so make up your mind to that!" He sprang toward her, laying his automatic on a table, and with a single gesture, it seemed to Iris, he had a soft silk handkerchief tied over her mouth, and around her head, in such fashion that she couldn't utter a sound.

"I'm sorry, as I told you," he went on, in a business-like voice, "but I *must* obtain that little piece of property. Will you change your mind and tell me where it is?"

Iris shook her head vigorously, meaning that she did not know where it was, but he chose to think she meant a mere negative.

"Then I'll make you!" and he took hold of her arm and twisted it. She moaned with pain, but he picked up the revolver and threatened her.

Iris was now really frightened, and realized that his gentler mood had passed, and she was in desperate danger. She cast appealing glances at him, but he was oblivious to her piteous eyes, and demanded the pin.

Suddenly the thought came to her that the man was crazy, really a maniac, and in view of this she determined to use her wits to extricate herself from this dangerous situation. If demented, he might shoot her as likely as not, and she thought deeply and carefully what it was best to do. He was distinctly clever, as she had heard maniacs often are, so she dared not fool him too openly.

Therefore, she acted rather defiantly, until, as she had hoped, this attitude on her part brought a rough, hard twist of her slender arm, that really brought the tears to her eyes.

With a limp gesture of surrender, she nodded her head at him, while pain contorted her face.

"Sorry," he said, again, "but there's no other way. Does that mean you're going to give me the pin?"

Iris nodded acquiescence, and he stipulated, "The real one?"

Again she nodded, salving her conscience by the thought that her falsehood was told in self-defence.

"Where is it? No, you needn't speak yet, indicate where it is, and I'll get it."

Iris nodded her head toward the desk, and the man went to it. He ran his fingers lightly over the various compartments, watching her the while, and as he touched one, she nodded.

She had remembered a small packet of papers, pinned with an old and somewhat rusty pin, and she determined to pass this pin off on him, if she could make herself dramatically convincing.

"I've always thought I could be an actress," the poor child said to herself, "now's my time to make good."

So, by dint of indicative nods and glances, she easily made her visitor discover the packet and the pin. The papers were valueless, and the pin, which held a paper band round them, was an ordinary, dull, old-looking one.

It was Iris' clever play of her eyes and her hands,— that betokened a great unwillingness to part with it, but did so under duress—that succeeded in making the thief believe it was the pin he was after. He scrutinized the papers, and threw them aside.

"A good hiding-place," he said, putting the papers back where they had been. "As obvious as Poe's 'Purloined Letter.' I don't ask you if this is *the* pin, for your speaking countenance has told me it is. I only bid you a very good evening."

He rose quickly, and without a further glance at Iris, he turned off the electric light on the table, and she heard him step softly through the living room, and out of one of the low windows that gave on to the verandah.

She sat where he had left her, not really in pain, but in some discomfort. Then, lifting her hands she managed to untie the handkerchief gag. It wasn't difficult, though the tight knot took a few moments to loosen.

She was tempted to turn on the light, and look at the silk handkerchief still in her hand, but she feared her visitor might discover the fraud and return.

She crept softly into the living room, closed and locked the window through which she had heard him go, and wondered whether it had been left unfastened or he had forced the catch. But that could wait till morning. She locked the living-room door on the hall side, for further safety, and returned to her room, determined to have additional bolts and bars attached here and there the next day.

Then she remembered the house was not hers, and though she might suggest she could not dictate.

Hours she lay awake, thinking it all over. In the security of her own room, she felt no fear and the dawn had begun to show before she slept.

"He's a crazy man," she told herself, finally, just as, at last, slumber came to her. "But it's queer the same mania attacked two people at the same time."

Next day she told Lucille Darrel the story.

"No, I don't think he was crazy," Miss Darrel said, "I think he's an agent of that other man, and they wanted to find out if you had given the first man the right pin. You see, when you made the second man—what's his name, Ashton?——"

"Yes, and the first was Pollock."

"Well, when Pollock doubted that you'd given him the right pin, he sent Ashton to find out, and then when you were so clever as to fool Ashton so fully, he thought you had been frightened into it, at last."

"But what do they want the pin *for*?"

"Just as Pollock said; to add to a collection of such things. You know that dime and pin joke is in all the papers. Everybody knows about it."

"But why so desperately anxious to get the very one? If they did have another, nobody would ever be the wiser."

"Not unless you withheld the real one, and then gave it or sold it to somebody else later. That would make Pollock's pin a fraud. Now, he's sure he has the very pin."

"Well, of all rubbish! But, you're right. I suppose friend Ashton went to the gate post, and not finding it there, he hovered around the house hoping to get in and hunt for himself."

"Just that. And he did get in—I'm not sure he wouldn't have taken something more valuable than the pin, if you hadn't caught him."

"I don't know; he didn't seem at all like an ordinary thief. Now, I'm going to see if Polly knows anything about the real pin."

* * * * *

It was nearly time for the Sunday dinner, and Iris, going to the kitchen, found the old cook busy with her preparations.

"Oh, don't bother me 'bout that now, Miss Iris," Polly said; "I've gotter set this custard——"

"Behave yourself, Polly! It won't hurt your old custard to take one minute to answer my question. Did you take a pin out of the under side of Agnes' pincushion?"

"Come outside here," and the cook drew Iris out to the kitchen porch. "Now," she whispered, "don't you talk so free 'bout that pin. Yes, Miss Iris, I got it, and you kin be mighty glad. That's a vallyble pin, that is, and don't you fergit it!"

"Valuable, how? And where is it?"

"Well, you know, Mrs. Pell, she set great store by that pin. Many's the time, when she's been goin' to New York or somewhere, she's said to me, 'Polly, you keep this safe till I get home,' and she'd hand me that self-same pin. And would I guard it? Well, wouldn't I!"

"But why, *why*, Polly, did she set such store by it?"

"It was her Luck, Miss Iris——"

"Luck, fiddlesticks! Aunt Ursula wasn't a fool! If she'd kept that pin for luck, she'd have stuck it away and left it alone."

"Now, you know there's no telling *what* Mrs. Pell would do! Anybody else might have done this or that, but there's no use sayin' *she* would. She was a law unto herself. But, anyway, that pin's valuable, and it don't matter for what reason! So, I got it away from Agnes, who hasn't a mite of right to it, and saved it for you. Why, Miss Iris, didn't your aunt, time and again, say she was goin' to leave you a valuable pin? Her little joke was neither here nor there. She said she'd leave you a *valuable* pin—and she did!"

"You're crazy too, Polly. Well, give me the pin; let me see if I can discover its great value. Perhaps if I rub it a Slave of the Pin will appear, to grant my wishes!"

"Here it is, Miss Iris," and Polly drew a pin from her bodice, "but for the land's sake be careful of it! Do, now!"

"I will, honest, I will," and Iris smiled as she took the common pin from the trembling fingers of the old woman.

"Lemme keep it for you, Miss Iris, dear. Won't you?"

"Maybe I will, later, Polly. I'll enjoy my valuable possession awhile, myself, first."

Iris went around the lawn toward the side door of the house. As she went, she looked curiously at the pin and then stuck it carefully in her shirtwaist frill.

As she neared the side door, she noticed a small motor car standing there. It was empty, and even as she looked, someone came up stealthily behind her, threw a thick, dark cloth over her head, picked her up and lifted her into the little car, and drove rapidly away.

She tried to scream, but a hand was held tightly over her mouth, and try as she would she could make no sound. She felt the familiar curve as they drove through the gateway, and turned off on the road that led away from the village, and Iris realized she was being kidnapped.

CHAPTER 10: FLOSSIE

When Iris failed to respond to the summons for dinner, Miss Darrel waited a few moments and then took her own place at the table.

"Go and find Miss Clyde," she said to Agnes; "I do wish people would be prompt at meals, especially when they're guests."

Lucille never allowed any one of her household to forget that she was now mistress of Pellbrook, and she longed for the time when the mystery would be cleared up and she might be left to the possession of her new home.

Being Sunday, it was a case of midday dinner, and, as Iris was usually prompt, Lucille was surprised at the length of time Agnes remained out of the room. At last she returned with the word that she could not find Miss Clyde anywhere in the house. "But," she added, "maybe she went away in the little car that was here a while ago."

"What little car?" demanded Lucille.

"I don't know whose it was, and I don't know that Miss Iris was in it, but I just caught sight of it as it whizzed through the gate."

"When?"

"About an hour ago. I didn't think much about it. I saw a man driving it, and I think there was a lady on the back seat——"

"Agnes, you're crazy! Miss Clyde wouldn't go out anywhere on Sunday morning without telling me. She didn't go to church?"

"Oh, no, ma'am, it was much too late for that."

"Well, that was some stranger's car. You didn't see Iris in it?"

"No, ma'am, I didn't."

However, as there was no Iris on the premises, Lucille Darrel concluded she had gone off on some sudden and unexpected errand—perhaps to see Winston Bannard.

So Miss Darrel ate her dinner alone, with no feeling of alarm, but a slight annoyance at the episode.

She thought over the story Iris had told her of the intruder of the night before, and slowly a vague suggestion of something wrong shaped itself in her brain. She realized that if Iris had gone on an errand, or had gone for a ride with Roger Downing, or any other friend or caller, she would certainly have told Lucille she was going. For Iris was punctilious in her courtesy, and the two women really got along very well together. She called old Polly in and asked her what she thought about it.

"I don't know," and the cook shook her head. "I'd just been talking to her about that pin Mrs. Pell left to her——"

"Good heavens! Polly! That pin again? Why—what *is* there about that pin? What do *you* know of it?"

"Well," and the old face was very serious, "I've been acquainted with that pin for years."

"Is it a special pin?"

"Very special."

"Why? What's its value?"

"That I don't know, ma'am, 'cept I'm thinking it's a lucky pin."

"Oh, how ridiculous! Why, you're not even sure the pin is in existence—I mean, that anybody knows of."

"Oh, yes, ma'am, I just gave that pin to Miss Iris this morning."

"*You* did! Where did you get it?"

"Well, I hooked it offen Agnes."

"What does this all mean? Why did you take it from Agnes? And where did she get it?"

"Well, Miss Darrel, ma'am, it's all mighty queer. I don't say's there's any such thing as luck, and then, I don't say as there isn't. Anyway, Mrs. Pell guarded that pin like everything while she was alive, and she left it to

Miss Iris when she died. Don't that look like it was a Luck?"

"Oh, that bequest business was a joke. Surely you know that."

"Not altogether it wasn't. The dime part was, maybe, but that pin—why, I *know* that pin, I tell you!"

"Do you mean you'd know that pin apart from a lot of other common pins?"

"No'm—I don't know as I can say that—but, well, maybe I could tell it."

"Polly, you're out of your head! But never mind all that now, tell me what you think of Miss Iris' absence? You know her. Would she run off anywhere just before dinner on Sunday, without telling anyone?"

"That she would not! Miss Iris is most considerate and thoughtful. She'd never go away without seeing you first."

"That's what I think. Then where is she?"

"I don't know, ma'am, but—but I'm—I'm awful scared!"

And flinging her apron over her face, as she burst into sobs, Polly ran out of the room.

Thoroughly alarmed, Lucille spoke again to Agnes.

"You're not *sure* you saw Miss Clyde in that car?"

"Oh, no, ma'am. I didn't see her at all. Only I didn't know the car, and I thought she might be in it. I know Mr. Downing's car, and Mr. Chapin's, and——"

"I think I'll telephone Mr. Chapin. What with murderings and maraudings this house is a frightful place! I almost wish it wasn't mine!"

She called Mr. Chapin on the telephone, and he came over as quickly as he could.

Then she told him of the intruder of the night before, and of the other efforts that had been made to get the pin.

The lawyer smiled. "Nonsense!" he said, "they're not after that pin! They're after something else."

"What?"

"I don't know, but probably the jewels, or memoranda or information as to where the jewels are."

"Where can they be?"

"I've not the slightest idea. I wish now I'd insisted more strongly on having Mrs. Pell's confidence. But she told me that her whole fortune was left to Iris and Win Bannard, and that it was all disclosed in the will's directions. She gave me to understand that the box for Iris and the pocket-book for Win held directions for the possessing of her fortune."

"Was her money all in the jewels?"

"All but a few shares of stock, and a little real estate. Those, however, will help along, for they belong to Iris and young Bannard as her immediate heirs, aside from her will."

"Well, I should think you would have insisted on knowing a little more about things than that!"

"Why should I? I drew her will, I attended to such matters as she asked me to, and it was not my affair where she chose to conceal her wealth, especially as she had given me a sealed box to hand over to her heiress at her death. And, too, Miss Darrel, you didn't know my late client as well as I did. Indeed, I doubt if many people knew her as I did! A lawyer often has queer clients, but I'm sure she set a record for eccentricities! I suppose I drew up a score of wills for her, and Lord knows how many codicils were added! Then, too, I never knew when she would perpetrate one of her silly jokes on me. I've been called over here late at night, to take her dying testamentary directions, only to arrive and find her perfectly well, and laughing at me! I've been given an extra fee for some trifling service, only to find that payment had been stopped at the bank before I could present the check."

"And you stood for such treatment?"

"What could I do? She was an old and valued client; she paid well, and the checks were always honored later, after she had had her fun out of me. And, of course, her tricks were merely tricks. She never did anything dishonest or dishonorable. Then, too, I liked the old lady.

Aside from her one foolish fad, she was intelligent and interesting. Oh, Ursula Pell was all right, except for that one bee in her bonnet. Now, I am perfectly certain her hoard of jewels is safely secreted and I think—I hope, she has left directions telling where they are. But if she hasn't, if, dying so unexpectedly, she has neglected to leave the secret, then I fear Iris will never get her inheritance. Why, they may be within a few feet of us, even now, and yet be so slyly hidden as to be irrecoverable."

"I think that's what the man was after last night."

"I daresay. But who was the man?"

"Not an ordinary burglar, for Iris declared he was a gentleman——"

"Gentlemen don't conduct themselves as——"

"You know what I mean! She said he was educated and cultured of speech and manner. Of course, he was a thief. He pretended he wanted the pin, but that was a blind. He was hunting the jewels."

"Well, *we'd* better hunt Iris. I don't like her unexplained disappearance. Suppose we telephone to all the people we can think of, at whose homes she might be."

But this procedure, though including the Bowens and many other of Iris' intimate acquaintances, brought forth positively no results. Nobody had seen or heard from Iris that day.

At last they telephoned to Hughes, and the detective said he would come to Pellbrook at once.

*   *   *   *   *

When Iris realized that she had been actually kidnapped, her feelings were of anger, rather than of fright. The indignity of the thing loomed above her sense of danger or fear of personal injury. The little car, a landaulet, ran smoothly and rapidly, and as soon as they were well away from Pellbrook the stifling cloth was partially removed from her head, and Iris discovered that beside her was a young woman, whose face, though determined, was not at all awe-inspiring. She even smiled at Iris' furious expression, and said, "Now, now, what's the use? You may as well take it quietly."

"Take kidnapping quietly!" blazed Iris. "Would *you?*"

"If I couldn't help myself any more than you can, yes."

"Keep still! Too much chattering back there!" came a voice from the driver's seat, and a scowling face turned round for a moment.

"All right," retorted Iris' cheerful companion, "you mind your business, and I'll mind mine."

Then, she took the covering entirely off Iris' head, but at the same time she drew down the silk shades to the windows of the car.

"Sorry," she said, blithely, "but it must be did!"

"Where am I? Where am I going?" and Iris frowned at her.

"You dunno where you're going, but you're on your way," sang the strange girl, for she was little more than a girl. "Now, don'tee fight—just take it pleasant-like, and it will be lots better for you."

"I don't care for your advice, thank you; I ask you what it means that I am forcibly carried off in this way?"

"It means we wanted you, see? Now, Miss Clyde—or, may I call you Iris?"

"You may not!"

"Oh, very well—ve-ry well! But you call me Flossie, won't you?"

"I've no desire to call you anything——"

"Fie, fie! What a temper! Or doesn't your common sense tell you that it would be better for you to make friends with me than not?"

"I reserve the privilege of choosing my own friends."

"Oho! Of course you do, usually. But this is an unusual incident. An out-of-the-way occurrence, if I may say so."

Iris preserved a stony silence.

"All right, Miss Clyde. Here's your last chance. Be a little more friendly with me, and I assure you you'll get off much more easily. Continue to rebuff me with these crool, *crool* glances, and—take the consequences!"

The last three words were said in such a menacing tone that Iris jumped. It seemed this laughing young woman could turn decidedly threatening.

Iris capitulated. "In view of what you imply, I'll be as friendly as I can, but I confess I don't feel really sisterly toward you!"

"That's better! That line o' talk is most certainly better. Now, maybe we can hit it off. What do you want to know?"

"Why I was carried off in this manner! Who did it? Where am I being taken? Why?"

"The questions put by thee, dear heart,
Are as a string of pearls to me——"

The lilting voice was true, and the soft tones very sweet. Iris was attracted, in spite of herself, to this strange person.

"I'll answer separately—every one apart——" she twittered on. "First, you were—ahem—accumulated, for a good and wise purpose. The principal actor, who could be said to answer your question of who did it, is not in our midst at present. You are being taken to a house. Why? Ah, if I tell you, you will know, won't you?"

Flossie looked provoking, but good-natured, and Iris deemed it wiser not to rouse her ire again.

"You haven't really answered, but I suppose you won't. Well, when can I go back home?"

"If you're goody-girl, you can return in, say, a couple of hours. If not—ah, if not!"

Suddenly a light broke upon Iris.

It was that pin! These strange people were after the pin!

And it was sticking in her shirtwaist frill, just where she had put it when Polly gave it to her. They must not get it! Now, if ever, she must use her wits. For, if anybody wanted that pin so desperately, it was, it *must be* valuable. Also, if Ursula Pell had cherished that pin as old Polly described, it surely was valuable.

Iris thought quickly. This sharp-eyed girl would be difficult to hoodwink, yet it must be done. Had she seen the pin? A furtive glance at the full ruffle of lawn and lace showed Iris that the pin was not prominently visible, though she could see it. Why did they want it? But that didn't matter now—now she must hide it. Would she be searched, she wondered. Surely she would not be submitted to such an insult. Yet, it might be. At any rate, it must be hidden. This was the real pin, the others had not been, and these people who were after it knew that. What the pin meant, or why they wanted it, must be left undecided, but the pin must be made safe.

Iris thought of dropping it out of the window, which was open, though the shade was down, but concluded that her ever finding it again would be too doubtful. She thought of concealing it in her abundant hair—but suppose she were made to take down her hair! A sort of intuition told her that she would be searched, and she must be ready.

At last she thought of a hiding-place, and as a start she drew Flossie's attention to a slightly loose shade tassel, while, with a gesture as of straightening a tiny velvet bow at her throat, she drew her hand down the frill, and brought the pin with it.

Concealed in her left hand, and stealthily watching her companion's eyes, she waited her chance, and then, unnoticed, she thrust it, head end first, into the hem of her white serge skirt. The loose weave of the material made this possible, and the pin disappeared into the inch wide hem. It might be safe there and it might not. Iris thought it would, and at any rate she could think of no better place to conceal it.

Also, getting another pin from her belt she placed it where the "valuable" pin had been, for further precaution.

Nor did she accomplish her work much too soon, for very shortly they drove in at a gate and stopped at the door of a small house.

There was no attempt at hiding now, and Iris was handed out of the car by the man who had driven them. With no appearance of stealth, Flossie ushered her into the house, which proved to be an ordinary, middle-class dwelling of country people.

The sitting room they went into had a table with a red cover, some books of no interest, and an old-fashioned lamp on a wool-work mat. The patent rocker and a few other worn chairs betokened family furnishings bought in the eighties, and not renewed since.

Flossie closed the door, and spoke to Iris, in a new and very decided tone.

"Miss Clyde," she said, with respect and politeness, "I'm truly sorry, but you are here and I am here, in order that I may take from you a pin, which you have somewhere in your clothing. I deeply regret the necessity, but it is imperative that I make sure of getting every pin that is on your person. Please do not make it harder for me—for both of us—than is necessary. For, I assure you, I shall do my duty."

"A pin?" said Iris, innocently, "here is one."

She took one from her belt, in which there chanced to be several, and thanked her lucky stars that she had hidden the real one. It might be found, for this girl was surely energetic, but Iris trusted much to her own dramatic ability now.

"Not one, but all," said Flossie, gravely. "I'm afraid you don't understand——"

"I'm sure I don't!" interrupted Iris. "What about a pin?"

"I won't waste words with you, if you please. I am here to take from you every pin you have in your clothing. You will please undress slowly, that I may get them all. Here is a paper of new ones to replace them. Will you please take off your shirtwaist, or shall I?"

Iris looked aghast. Then she concluded it would be best to submit.

"Will you lock the door?" she said, haughtily.

"It is locked. We are quite safe from intrusion or interruption. Please proceed."

Iris proceeded. But as she removed her shirtwaist, she furtively, yet careful that Flossie should see her, glanced at the pin in its frill. She laid the garment on a chair, and went on to disrobe, with the cold dignity of a queen on the scaffold.

Flossie was kind and delicately courteous.

"Not your underclothing, of course," she said. "I have reason to think you secreted the pin I want in your clothes, a few moments before you—before you left home, and I think it must be in your frock or petticoats. Or, perhaps, in your camisole."

She examined the dainty lingerie with scrutinizing care, and extracted every pin—of which she found several. Each one she carefully laid aside, and gravely offered Iris a new pin in its place.

Pretty sure, now, that her pin would not be found, Iris let herself be amused at the whole performance.

"Do you do this as a profession," she asked, "or are you an amateur?"

"Both," was the unsmiling answer. "Will you give me your word there are no more pins on you?"

"I will give you my word there is only this one, and you are welcome to it." Iris took a pin from a loop of ribbon that adorned her petticoat ruffle, "but I must ask for one to replace it. I'm a shockingly careless mortal, and I fully meant to sew that bow on, but I didn't."

Flossie stared at her hard, but Iris didn't quiver an eyelash of fear or apprehension, and the other allowed her to dress herself again.

"That is all," Flossie said, shortly, as once more Iris was in full costume. "We will go now."

They re-entered the car, which was still at the door, and started back the way they had come.

CHAPTER 11: GONE AGAIN!

"The murder mystery is bad enough," said Hughes, "but this disappearance of Miss Clyde is also alarming. There is deep deviltry going on, and since Winston Bannard is in custody it can't be assumed that he had any hand in the matter."

"Unless Iris is doing something for Win," suggested Miss Darrel.

"They may be working in collusion——" began Hughes, but Mr. Chapin interrupted. "Don't use such an expression! Working in collusion implies wrong-doing. If those two, or either of them, should be hunting the hidden jewels, they have a perfect right to do so. The jewels belong to them—if they can find them."

"Iris Clyde isn't on any jewel hunt," declared Hughes, when, at that very moment, in at the door came Iris herself.

Her hair was decidedly tumbled, and her pretty lingerie waist was rumpled, but otherwise she looked trim and tidy.

But angry! Her eyes blazed as she cried, "Oh, I am so glad you men are here! I've had such an experience! Mr. Hughes, you must look up the people who kidnapped me—kidnapped me, in broad daylight! At my own side door! It seems to me as incredible as it must seem to you!"

"There, there," said Lucille, trying to calm the excited girl, "have you had your dinner?"

"No, and I don't want any. Listen, everybody, while I tell you about it."

They listened, breathlessly and absorbedly, while Iris told every detail of her adventure.

"And then," she wound up, "after Flossie had searched me as thoroughly as a police matron might have done, she allowed me to put on my things again, and we came back just as we went. I mean, I was put into the car with her, it was a little coupe affair, you know, and the same man drove it. We had the shades up part of the time, but as we made a turn she pulled them down, and as we neared this house, she put the shawl over my head again. It was a nice, white, woolly shawl, and smelt faintly of violet. Well, when we got to the bend of the—road below here, they asked me to get out and walk the rest of the way. I did so, gladly enough! I was so relieved to see the house again, that I just *ran* to it. They scooted, of course, and that's all. Now, Mr. Hughes, catch 'em!"

"Not so easy, Miss Clyde. The thing was carefully planned, and carried out with equal care. Did they get the pin?"

"They did not! Now, Mr. Hughes—Mr. Chapin, that pin must have some value. What can it be? To say it's a lucky pin is silly, I think."

"But what else could be its value?" said Chapin, wonderingly. "Let me see it."

"I won't let anybody see it, unless we draw the blinds and lock the doors," said Iris, decidedly. "I tell you there is some value to this pin. Could it be made of radium, or something like that?"

"Let's see it," demanded Hughes.

"All right, I will," and Iris locked the doors herself, and drew down the window shades. Then, turning on an electric light, she turned up the hem of her white serge skirt, and began feeling for the pin. And she found it, though the point had come through the material. But the head held it in, and Iris easily extricated it.

"There!" she said, holding it up, "that is the 'valuable pin' Aunt Ursula bequeathed to me. What do you make of it?"

Hughes took it first, and looked at it curiously. "Just a common, ordinary pin," he said, "no radium about that."

"Did you ever see any radium?" asked Iris.

"No; but I've seen common pins all my life, and that's one."

"Of course it is;" and Lucille Darrel's positive statement rather settled the matter.

Mr. Chapin looked at it, but could see nothing unusual about it. It was not bright, like a new pin, yet it was not yellowed with age. It was merely a *pin*, and nothing more could be made of it.

"It's a blind," said Hughes, with conviction. "Those people, whoever they may be, pretend they're after this pin, but really they think you have a real diamond pin left you by your aunt, and they're after that."

"That might be," agreed Chapin. "Did the search indicate anything of the sort, Iris?"

"I can't say. If so, at least, that girl made a big bluff of hunting an ordinary pin. I tried to fool her. I had put a pin of hers in the frill of my blouse, and I kept looking toward it, but furtively, as if eluding her attention. She caught on, and she examined that frill in every plait! She found the pin I had put there, of course, and she took special care of it, though pretending it was of no particular importance. I put one, as if hidden, in my petticoat ruffle, too, and she fairly pounced on that, but she gave me a glance to see if I noticed her satisfaction! Oh, we played our parts, and it was diamond cut diamond, I can tell you. I couldn't help liking her; she's really a nice girl, and she must have been made, or hired, to do what she did. She made me take down my hair, and she brushed it herself, in hope of finding a pin in it! And I did think of hiding it there at first, but I thought it safer where I put it. You see, it couldn't lose out, and there was little likelihood of her thinking to feel in the hem of my skirt."

"Very well done; you're a heroine, Miss Clyde, indeed you are! But, I fear the end is not yet. When they find they haven't the right pin——"

"How can they possibly know?" exclaimed Miss Darrel. "How can they tell that they haven't?"

"They must be able to tell, because they were not satisfied with the pins Mr. Pollock took from here."

"Pollock!" cried Iris. "It wasn't Pollock who ran that car to-day."

"No, but it's his affair. He sent the little car for you——"

"How did he know I'd be out there and with the pin in my possession?"

"He's been on the watch, all day, likely. Oh, you don't know the cleverness of a really clever villain. But give me an idea which way you went."

"I have no idea. You see, all the time the shades were up the shawl was over my head, and when she took the shawl off I couldn't see out at all."

"You've no notion what road you traveled?"

"Not a bit, after we left this place. I think they made unnecessary turns, for the car turned around often."

"You see what clever rascals we have to deal with?" grumbled Hughes. "And you recognized no landmarks?"

"Not one."

"What was the house like?"

"Fairly nice; old-fashioned, but not antique at all. Decent furnishings, but no taste, and nothing of real value. Commonplace, all through."

"The hardest kind of a house to trace!"

"Yes, there was nothing distinctive at all."

"No people in it?"

"Not that I know of. I heard no sound. Flossie took me into a little sitting room to undress, not a bedroom. Everything was clean, but ordinary. Of course, I'd know the room if I saw it again, but I've no glimmering of an idea where it was."

"Strangest case I ever heard of!" mused Mr. Chapin. "I think the pin has some especial value. Maybe it is of gold, inside."

"Nonsense!" said Lucille, scornfully, "that amount of gold wouldn't be worth anything! I'm inclined to the radium theory, though I don't know a thing about the stuff."

"Well, I'm going to hide this pin, right now," said Iris, "and I want you all to see where I put it. I'm afraid to put it in the bank or in Mr. Chapin's safe, for those people would get it somehow. But here are only Mr. Chapin and Mr. Hughes and Miss Darrel and myself. We are all trustworthy, and I'll hide it. Then, I shall devote my life to the solving of the mystery of the pin and Aunt Ursula's death—for, I think they are very closely connected."

"I believe you!" cried Hughes, "and I agree that the best place to hide the thing is in this house. Where, now?"

"In Auntie's room," said Iris, solemnly, and she led the way to Ursula Pell's sitting room. "This place is barred and we can lock the door to the other room, and keep it locked. See, I shall put it in this big easy chair, that Auntie loved to sit in. I'll tuck it well down in between the back and the seat upholstery, and no one can find it. Then, if we ever discover wherein its value lies, we know where the pin is, and can get it."

"I suppose that's all right," said Mr. Chapin, a little dubiously, "but in a safe——"

"No, Miss Clyde's idea is best," asserted Hughes. "How cleverly she hid the thing in her skirt hem, didn't she? Let her alone for the right dope about this. As she says, we four know where it is, and that's all that's necessary. I believe the people who want this pin will stick at nothing, and if it's in any ordinary safe they'll get it."

"But what *could* they want of it?" repeated Lucille, plaintively. "Just as a surmise, what *could* they want of it?"

"I'll tell you!" cried Iris, with a flash of inspiration. "It's a clue or a key to where the jewels are hidden! Oh, it must be! That's why they want it!"

"Clue? How?" said Lucille, in bewilderment.

"I don't know, but, say, the pin is the length of—of——"

"I don't know what you're getting at," said Chapin, "but all pins are the same length."

"What!" cried Hughes, "indeed they're not!"

"Oh, well, I mean there are only a few lengths. The pins that girl took from Iris to-day are just the same as this one, aren't they?"

"About," said Iris; "of course, pins differ, but the ones we use are generally of nearly the same length. But I'm sure the length or weight of this pin——"

"Weight!" exclaimed Hughes; "suppose a certain weight, goldsmith's scales, you know—would open a delicately adjusted lock on a safe——"

"You're romancing, man," and Mr. Chapin smiled, "but it does seem that the pin must have some significance. It would be just like Ursula Pell to call it a valuable pin, when it really was a valuable pin, in some such sense as a key to a hiding-place."

"But how?" repeated Lucille; "I don't see how its weight or length could be a key——"

"Nor I," agreed Hughes, "but I believe it is, all the same! I've a lot of confidence in Miss Clyde's intuition, or insight, or whatever you choose to call it. And I believe she's on the right track. I confess I can't see how, but I do think there may be some connection between this pin and the hidden jewels——"

"But what good does it do, if we can't find it?" objected Lucille.

"We will find it," declaimed Iris, her eyes shining with strong purpose, "we must find it. And if we do, we'll be indebted to these people for putting us on the right track."

"They'll probably turn up again, pin-hunting," mused Mr. Chapin.

"Let 'em!" said Iris, scornfully, "I'm not afraid of them. They're determined, Lord knows! But they're not dangerous."

"They gagged you——"

"But not in a ruffianly manner! No, I'm not afraid. If Miss Darrel will let me stay here a while longer, I believe I can ferret out——"

"Stay as long as you like, dear child," and Lucille smiled kindly on her, "and I'll help you. I'm fond of puzzles, myself, and maybe I can help more than you'd think!"

"Now, I want to go and see Win, and tell him all about it," Iris announced; "mayn't I?"

"I think I can arrange that——" began Hughes; but Lucille said, "Not now, Iris, you must have some food first. Why, you've had no dinner at all, and it's after four o'clock!"

"I'm not hungry," Iris insisted, but Miss Darrel carried her off to the dining room.

"Mighty queer mix-up," Hughes said to the lawyer.

"It is so, but I can't think there's any importance to that pin. These theories don't hold water."

"I dunno's they do, but they've got to be looked into. That pin's safe for the present, I think, safer'n it'd be in a bank. That is, unless somebody was lookin' in the window. Miss Clyde was mighty careful to draw the shades in the other room, but she forgot it in here—and so did I."

"Oh, there's nobody to look in. The house is so far back from the road, and none of the servants are of the prying sort."

"That's all very well, but I believe in taking every precaution. Say, Mr. Chapin, has it ever struck you that Win Bannard might be in cahoots with these pin people?"

"Winston? Good heavens, no! What do you mean?"

"Well, nothing in particular, but you know I arrested Bannard because I thought he killed his aunt—and I've had no reason to change my mind."

"How——"

"Don't say 'how did he get out?' Just remember that the murderer *did* get out, and we must find him first, and then he'll tell us how."

"Oh, not Win Bannard!"

"Then, who? Who else had motive, opportunity, and— well, you know his finances are in a bad way?"

"No, I didn't know it."

"Well, they are. And he told some of his pals in New York on Saturday night that he'd touch his aunt for five thousand on Sunday! How's that?"

"Did he really?"

"He really did. And we've more counts against him, too. Oh, Winston Bannard has a lot to explain! But I don't want to talk here. These are state secrets."

"But tell me, how did you find out so much about Bannard?"

"By inquiries I got afoot, and they panned out pretty good. Why, I've got a witness to prove that he stopped at the Red Fox Inn that Sunday, just as he said he did, but it was on his way *up* here, not on his way *back*, as he declares!"

"Hughes, that's bad!"

"Bad? You bet it is! I'm sorry for Bannard, but I've got to track him down. I'll be going now; I've a heap to see to. Tell the ladies good-bye for me."

The detective went off and Lawyer Chapin, with the privilege of a family friend, went to the dining room, where Iris was trying to eat, all the while excitedly telling Lucille further details of the kidnapping affair.

"I'm terribly interested," Miss Darrel was saying, "and I want you to stay here, Iris, till it's all cleared up. And I want to get a big detective up from the city. I don't think very much of Hughes, do you, Mr. Chapin?"

"Not much, no. But big detectives are very expensive."

"If one can find Iris' inheritance, she won't mind the cost."

"And if he doesn't succeed?"

"Then I'll pay it!" Lucille spoke positively and with a determined shake of her head. "I've money of my own, and I'll pay if he doesn't find the jewels, and if he does Iris can reward me, eh, girlie?"

"Of course I will! Oh, Lucille, do you mean it? I'm so glad. You know Win isn't guilty, I know he isn't, and a fine detective could find out who is, and how he did the murder, and then he can find the jewels, and everything will be cleared up!"

"Don't go too fast," cautioned Chapin, "even a great detective would find this a hard case, I'm sure."

"But if he fails, Miss Darrel will pay his fee, and if he succeeds, I will, and gladly! And I'll give you a big present too," she added glancing brightly at Lucille.

"Now, I'm going to see Win," Iris went on, pushing back from the table, "but first, let's talk over this detective matter." She led the way back to the sitting room, which had come to be the general rendezvous for discussions.

She looked around the room, thoughtfully. "If we have a detective," she said; "he'll ask first of all if anything has been touched. The place hasn't been much disturbed, has it?"

"Very little," agreed Lucille. "And we can be careful that nothing else is touched."

"And I'm going to pick up and put away anything that can be considered a clue." Iris took up the old pocket-book, as she spoke. "We've all looked on this as no account, because the contents are missing; perhaps the detective will be interested in the empty pocket-book."

"Then there's the New York paper," suggested Lucille.

Iris winced. "They think that implicates Win," she said, slowly, "but I don't! So I'm going to take that, too. The cigarette stub Mr. Hughes took away with him. But everybody smokes that brand. Now, what else?"

"The check-book," said Chapin, gravely. "Be careful, Iris. Everything does seem to point to Win, you know."

"It seems to, yes, but does it? You know yourself, Mr. Chapin, anybody might have a New York Sunday paper— oh, well, I'm going ahead, because I know Win is innocent, and these seeming clues may help to find the real villain."

"Good stuff, you are, Iris!" declared the lawyer, looking at her admiringly. "Go in and win!"

"Win for Win!" and Iris smiled brightly.

"Are you in love with him?" cried Lucille, who had not thought of such a thing.

"Yes," said Iris, simply. "Now, Mr. Chapin, are you going to help me?"

"Certainly I am, if I can. How?"

"Well, first of all, I've changed my mind about that pin. I don't think I'll leave it where it is. I did think it wise, but it seems to me that anyone searching thoroughly, desperately, would look in the chair cushions, and so, I think I'll ask you to put it in your safe, but— don't tell Mr. Hughes we've changed its hiding-place."

"Very well, Iris; the pin is certainly yours, and if you give it to me for safe-keeping, I'll do my best to protect it."

"And don't tell Mr. Hughes, for he's liable to want to see what it's made of. I'll give it to you now."

"Draw the shades first, don't fail to use every precaution. That's right; I'll switch on a light. Why do you have this table light on this long cord?"

"It was put in lately, and it was less trouble to do it that way. Now I'll get the pin. It does seem ridiculous to make such a fuss over a pin!"

"Here's a little box," said Mr. Chapin, taking an empty one from the desk, "we can put it in this."

"Why, where is it?" said Iris, looking blank. "I stuck it right in this corner."

But the pin was gone!

Search as they would, in the soft cushions, there was no pin there. Nor had it sunk through the upholstery material. The closely woven brocade would not permit of that. They faced the astounding fact—the pin was gone!

CHAPTER 12: IN CHICAGO

The three looked at one another in consternation.

"Hughes said it was unsafe," Chapin remarked. "He said you didn't remember to pull down the shades in this room when you hid the pin, Iris."

"No, I didn't, but who could get in? The windows are barred——"

"But the door to the living room was open, and we were all in the dining room—anyone could have come in at the front door and walked in here——"

"Very silently, then, or we could have heard footsteps from the dining room."

"But it must have been done that way. Someone looking in at these windows saw you put the pin in the chair, and a few moments later, watching his chance, sneaked in and stole it."

"Then it was Pollock, or some messenger of his. But what *can* he want of it?"

"The whole thing is *too* mysterious!" exclaimed Lucille. "Let's send for a city detective at once."

"But," objected Iris, "what could he do?"

"Do? He could do everything! Find the murderer, find the jewels, find the pin——"

"Good gracious!" cried Iris. "I don't want the pin! In fact, I'm glad it's gone. Now, they won't be kidnapping me to get it! But I'm going to find the jewels. And I'm going to start on a new tack. I'm no good at solving mysteries, but I can investigate. I'm going to Chicago——"

"Whatever for?" exclaimed Lucille; "I'll go with you!"

"No; I'm going alone, and I'm going because I feel sure I can find out something there. I'll see the minister of the church Auntie attended, and see if she promised him a chalice, or if his church has a crypt, or if those people she spoke of in her will—that firm, you know—can tell me anything about the receipt that was in the pocket-book she left to Win."

"But it wasn't in the pocket-book!" reminded Chapin.

"It was when Aunt Ursula made that will. The murderer took it, and, Mr. Chapin, that lets Win out! Why should he steal a paper that was meant for him anyway?"

"He didn't know then that it was left to him, did he?"

"I don't know that, I'm sure. But I know Win didn't kill Aunt Ursula, and it's awful to keep him shut up!"

"I think myself they hardly had enough evidence to arrest him on, but Hughes thought they did, and the district attorney is hard at work on the case now."

"Yes, hard at work!" Iris spoke scornfully, "what's he doing, I'd like to know."

"These things move slowly, Iris——"

"Well, I'll do a little quick work, then, and show them how. I'm going to Chicago to-morrow, and I'll be gone several days, but I'll be back as soon as possible and there'll be something doing, or I'll know why!"

"Your energy is all right, Iris," said Chapin, "but a bit misdirected——"

"Nothing of the sort," snapped Iris, who considered the lawyer an old fogy; "it's time somebody got busy, and I don't take much stock in the local police."

"But about the pin," pursued Lucille, "I think you ought to find out who stole it just now, Iris. Maybe it was somebody in the house. Where is Purdy?"

"Purdy!" cried Iris, "don't suspect him, Lucille! Why, he is as faithful and honest as I am myself."

"But where was he?"

"I don't know, and I don't care; he wasn't in here stealing the pin."

"Perhaps it's still in the chair," suggested Chapin.

But it wasn't. A careful search showed that, and as inquiries proved that Purdy and his wife were in the kitchen and Agnes had been waiting on Iris at her belated dinner, there was really no reason to suspect the servants. Campbell, the chauffeur, was in the garage, and there were no other servants about on Sunday. The disappearance of the pin was as inexplicable as the murder, and Iris decided to give up the house mysteries, and look in Chicago for new light.

* * * * *

She started the next day, Lucille and Agnes hovering over her in a solicitude of final preparations.

"I'll take only a suitcase," Iris declared, "for I can't be bothered with a trunk."

"I wish you'd let Agnes go with you," urged Lucille, who hated to have the girl go alone.

But Iris didn't want to take a maid along, and, too, Agnes didn't want to go.

"I'll go if you say so," Agnes demurred, "but I'd hate to leave here just now. Sam is on one of his spells, and I ought to look after him."

"Oh, yes," and Iris smiled at her, "that's one word for Sam and two for yourself! I think that good-looking young man who calls on you has more power to keep you in Berrien than poor Sam!"

Agnes blushed, but didn't deny it.

So Iris went to Chicago alone. She went to a woman's hotel, and established herself there. Then she set out in search of the church that Mrs. Pell used to attend.

The rector, Dr. Stephenson, was a kindly, courteous old man, who received her with a pleasant welcome. He well remembered Ursula Pell, and was deeply interested in the mystery of her tragic death. It was many years since she had lived in Chicago, and his definite memories of her were largely concerning the pranks she used to play, for even the minister had not been spared her annoying fooleries.

But he knew nothing of any gift of a jeweled chalice, and said he really had no desire for such a thing.

"It would only be a temptation to thieves," he asserted, "and the price of it could be much better expended in some more useful way."

"Is there a crypt in your church?" asked Iris, abruptly.

"No; nothing of the sort. Or—well, that is, there is a room below the main floor that could be called a crypt, I suppose, but it is never used as a chapel, or for mortuary purposes. Why?"

Iris told him of the entry in her aunt's diary stating that the collection of jewels was in a crypt, and Dr. Stephenson smiled.

"Not in my church," he said, "of that I'm positive. The basement I speak of has no hidden places nor has anybody ever concealed anything there. You may search there if you choose, but it is useless. To my mind, it sounds more like a bank vault. That might be called a crypt, if one chose so to speak of it."

"Perhaps," said Iris, disappointed at this fruitless effort. "I will go to the Industrial Bank and inquire. That is the bank where my aunt kept her money when she lived here."

The people at the bank were also kind and courteous, but not so much at leisure as the rector had been. They gave Iris no encouraging information. They looked up their records, and found that Mrs. Pell had had an account with them some years ago, but that it had been closed out when she left the city. There were no properties of hers, of any sort, in their custody, and no one of their vaults was rented in her name.

They seemed uninterested in Iris' story, and after their assurances the girl went away.

Next she went to the firm of Craig, Marsden & Co., to see if she could trace the receipt that was mentioned in Mrs. Pell's will as being of importance to Winston Bannard.

A Mr. Reed attended to her errand.

"A vague description," he said, smiling, as she told him of the will. "To be sure, our books will show the name, but it will take some time to look it up."

However, he agreed to investigate the records, and Iris was told to return the next day to learn results.

It was a mere chance that the record of the sale, whatever it might be, would be of any definite importance, but Iris was determined to try every possible way of finding out anything concerning the matter.

The firm of Craig, Marsden & Co. was a large jewelry concern, and probably the receipt in question was for some precious stones or their settings.

Iris boarded a street car to return to her hotel. She sat, deeply engrossed in thought over the various difficulties that beset her path, when the man who sat next her drew a handkerchief from his pocket.

Abstractedly, she noticed the handkerchief. It was of silk, and had a few lines of blue as a border. Then, suddenly, she realized that it was the exact counterpart of the one with which the midnight marauder had tied up her mouth the time he came to get the pin.

Furtively she glanced at the man. The burglar had been masked, but the size and general appearance of this man were not unlike him. Then, another surreptitious look revealed his features to her, and to her surprise she recognized her caller named Pollock!

Quickly she turned her own face aside (the man had not noticed her) and wondered what to do. Without a doubt it was Pollock, she was sure of that, and the peculiar handkerchief gave her an idea it was the midnight intruder also—that they were one and the same! She had surmised this before, and she now began to join the threads of the story.

She felt sure that Pollock and the burglar and the kidnapper were all one, and that Pollock was determined to get the pin at any cost; and she couldn't believe it was for the reason he had asserted, merely as a memento of the dramatic tragedy.

It had not been this man who drove the little car that carried her away on Sunday, but the driver, as well as the girl called Flossie, were probably Pollock's tools.

At any rate, she concluded to trace Pollock and find out something about him.

When he left the car, as he did shortly, she rose and followed him. He had not glanced at her, and was apparently absorbed in thought, so she had no difficulty in walking, unnoticed, behind him.

She smiled at herself, as she realized she was really "shadowing," and felt quite like a detective.

Pollock went into a small restaurant, and Iris, through the wide window, saw him take a seat at a table. The deliberation with which he unfolded his napkin, and looked over the menu, made her assume that he would be there some time.

Acting on the impulse of the moment, Iris ran to the nearest telephone she could find, and called up a detective agency.

Over the wire she stated her desire to employ a detective at once, and asked to have him sent to her, where she was, which was in a drug shop.

There was a maddening delay, and as Iris waited, she began to fear she had done a foolish thing. She suddenly realized that she had acted too quickly and perhaps unadvisedly. But she must stand by it now.

It was half an hour before a man arrived and met her at the door of the drug shop.

"I am Mr. Dayton," he said, "from the agency. Is this Miss Clyde?"

"Yes," said Iris, "and please hurry! I've just got on the track of a man who is a—a burglar——"

"Ma'am?" and the detective looked sharply at this young girl who had called him to her.

"Yes," and Iris grew impatient at his doubtful interest, "now, don't stop to parley, but catch him."

"Where is he?"

"He's in the restaurant, half a block away. I don't mean for you to arrest him, but trail him, shadow him, or whatever you call it, and find out who he is, and what sort of a character he bears. If he's a correct and decent citizen, all right; if he's a man who might be a burglar, I want to know it! Now, fly!"

"Wait a minute, Miss Clyde. Tell me more. How shall I know him?"

"Oh, he's at the table by the first front window, as you go from here. He's a tall man, and a strong-looking one. Come on, I'll point him out."

They went toward the restaurant, and cautiously Iris looked in at the window. But her quarry had fled. There was no one at the table at all.

"Come on in," she cried to the bewildered Dayton. "No, that won't do, he mustn't see me. You go in, and get the waiter who served him, or the proprietor or somebody, and find out who the man was who ate at that table just now. Maybe he's still in the coat room."

Iris stepped around a corner, and Dayton went in on his errand.

But the waiter had no knowledge of the patron's name. He said he had never seen him before, to his knowledge, but he was a new waiter there, and the captain might know.

However, neither the head waiter nor the cashier, nor indeed anyone about the place, knew the man. A few remembered seeing him, but the waiters at nearby tables, if they had noticed him, didn't know his name.

One waiter said he thought he had seen him before, but wasn't sure. The man was gone, and no one knew which direction he had taken from the restaurant.

Iris was disheartened at the report of her emissary.

"If you'd only got here sooner!" she reproached the detective.

"Did my best," he assured her. "Describe your man more accurately."

But Iris couldn't seem to think of any very distinguishing characteristics that fitted him.

"His name is Pollock," she said, "and he's a collector. Oh, wait, I do know something more. He's in the hardware business."

"For himself, or with a firm?"

"I don't know."

"Then, I fear, Miss Clyde, we're wasting time in looking for a person so vaguely identified. If you say so, I can go over the hardware people for a Pollock, but it will be an unsatisfactory and expensive process."

"I don't want that," and Iris looked perplexed. "Oh, I don't know what I *do* want! But it's maddening to see him, and then have him get away! He's also a collector."

"Ah, that helps. A collector of what?"

"Of mementoes of crimes——"

"Of what?"

"It sounds silly, I know, but he told me so. Not exactly crimes, more of prominent people. Like a pencil that belonged to President Garfield, and such things."

"Oh, a freak! I hoped you meant a prominent collector of valuable things; then we might trace him."

"No; he collects queer things, it is a sort of harmless mania, I think. Well, if we can't find him, we can't. How much do I owe you?"

This matter was adjusted, and Iris turned disconsolately back to her hotel. She had accomplished nothing on her Chicago trip, and unless the Craig people could give her information of importance, there was no use prolonging her visit.

The rest of that day, and the morning of the next, she spent in the vicinity of the restaurant, hoping Pollock would return.

But she didn't see him, and in the afternoon she went back to Craig, Marsden & Co.

Mr. Reed greeted her pleasantly, but he had no important information.

"We've many records of sales to Mrs. Pell," he related, "and, if you desire, I can give you a memorandum of them. Presumably, she had receipts in every case, but as I do not know the particular receipt you want, I can't offer you any data concerning it."

"What are the transactions?" asked Iris. "Jewels she bought?"

"Yes; and setting, and engraving. Mrs. Pell had a great deal of engraving done."

"What sort of engraving?"

"On silver or gold trinkets and ornaments."

"Oh, yes, I know. All her silver has not only initials, but names and dates, and sometimes quotations or lines of poetry."

"Yes, and she was most particular about that work. It was always done by our best engraver, and unless it just suited her we were treated to her finest sarcasm. Mrs. Pell was a wealthy and extravagant patron, but not affable or easy to please."

"I know that, but she was a remarkable woman and a strong character often has peculiar ways. I am heir to half her fortune, and that gives me a sense of obligation that will never be canceled until I have avenged my aunt's death."

Iris did not tell this man about the missing jewels, for it seemed of no use. But they discussed at length the jewels that he knew that Mrs. Pell had possessed, and Iris was amazed at the size and value of the amount.

"Really!" she exclaimed. "Do you *know* that my aunt had such an enormous fortune as that, in gems?"

"I know that she had at the time of her dealings with us. That was ten years ago, or so, but then we had the handling of more than a million dollars' worth, and I know she added to her store after that."

"Oh, where are they?" cried Iris forgetting her determination not to discuss this matter here.

"Do you mean to say you don't know?" exclaimed Mr. Reed, astounded.

So Iris told him about the will.

"What an extraordinary tale," he commented as she finished. "I wish I could help you out, I'm sure. Now, no receipt of ours would be of importance in and of itself. It must have had a memorandum scribbled on it, or something of that sort."

"Yes," agreed Iris, thoughtfully, "that must be it. In that case the murderer wanted it because it told where the jewels are hidden."

"And he has already secured them! Oh, no!"

Mr. Reed's interest was so sincere that Iris told him a little more. She told him of the pin, and of her being kidnapped in an attempt to get it.

"You are in danger," Reed said, warningly. "Until they get what they want you will continue to be molested. It isn't the pin—that's too absurd! But they're after something that has to do with the secret of the hiding place of those jewels. On that you may depend."

"But couldn't the pin have some bearing on that?"

"I can't imagine any way that it could. The idea of its being made of radium is ridiculous. The idea of its being a weight or a measure is silly, too; and how else could it be indicative? No, the pin part of the performance is a ruse, the thieves are after something else. If they stole the receipt in question, it was, as I said, because there were instructions on it. Your man Pollock is doubtless the head of the gang. He's no important collector, or I should know of him. And probably his whole collection story was a falsehood. He read of the pin in the paper and used that to distract your mind from what he really was after."

"Very likely," and Iris sighed. "What would you advise me to do?"

"It's too big a case for a layman's advice, and, pardon me, too big a case for a young girl to manage."

"Oh, I know that. I've a very good lawyer, and the police are at work, but nobody seems able to accomplish anything."

"I hope and trust somebody will," said Reed, heartily; "that lot of jewels is too big a loot for crooks to get hold of! I'd be sorry indeed to learn they have done so!"

Iris went away, and as her work in Chicago was done, she decided to start at once for home.

Entering the hotel, she found a telegram from Lucille Darrel. It read:

"Come home at once. I've engaged F. S. and he will arrive to-morrow."

Now, F. S. meant the great detective, Fleming Stone.

CHAPTER 13: FLEMING STONE COMES

Fleming Stone carried his years lightly. Except for the slight graying at his temples, no one would think that he had arrived, as he had, at the years that are called middle-aged.

But an especially interesting problem so stirred his enthusiasm and roused his energies that he grew young again, and his dark eyes fairly scintillated with eagerness and power.

"Tell me everything," he repeated, even after he had heard all the details over and over again. "Omit nothing—no tiniest point. It all helps."

They sat in the living room at Pellbrook, Miss Darrel and Iris being present, also Hughes and Lawyer Chapin.

Stone had examined the sitting room where Mrs. Pell had died, and, closing its door, had returned to the big living room, for further information on the whole subject of the crime and its subsequent events.

"The pin's the thing," he said, at last. "Everything hinges on that."

"Do you think so?" asked Mr. Chapin. "It seems to me the pin's a blind—a decoy—and the people hunting it are really after something else, of intrinsic value."

Fleming Stone looked at the lawyer, with a courteous impatience.

"No, Mr. Chapin, the pin is the thing they are after. It was for that pin that Mrs. Pell was murdered. That is why her dress was torn open at the throat, the villain was searching for that pin. That's why the desk was ransacked, the handbag explored, the pocket-book emptied—all in a desperate effort to find that seemingly insignificant pin! That why the poor woman was tortured, maltreated, bruised and beaten, in final attempts to make her tell where the pin was. Failing, the wretch flung her to the floor, in a burst of murderous frenzy."

"That's why I was kidnapped, then," exclaimed Iris.

"Of course, and you may be again! Those people will stop at nothing! The letters asking for the pin, the caller who wanted it for his 'collection,' all represent the same master-mind, who is after the pin.

"But why?" wondered Hughes, "what do they want of the pin?"

"The pin means the jewels," declared Stone, briefly. "How, I can't say, exactly, for the moment, but the pin is the open sesame to the hiding-place of the gems, and only the possession of it will secure the treasure. We must get the pin—and then, all else will be clear sailing."

"But the pin is gone," lamented Iris.

"That is the worst phase of it all," Stone said, regretfully. "It is such a difficult thing to trace—not only so tiny, and easily lost, but so like thousands of others, that it can't readily be discerned even if seen."

"You think it's just an ordinary pin, then?" inquired Chapin.

"Absolutely, sir."

"Then why won't any other pin do as well?"

Stone looked at him keenly. "I can't answer that at present, Mr. Chapin; my theory regarding the pin, while doubtless the truth, is as yet uncertain. Now, another and equally great problem is that of the murderer's exit. From your story of the crime, I gather that the room was absolutely unenterable, except by breaking in the door, which Purdy and the chauffeur did?"

"That is true," agreed Iris; "the windows, as you can see, are strongly barred, and there is but the one door. Search has been made for secret entrances or concealed passages, but there is nothing of the sort."

"No," said Stone, "this sort of a house is not apt to have such. If there were any, they would be easily discovered. And there were several people in this room, when the two men burst in the door?"

"Yes," said Iris. "I was here, and Polly, the cook, and the two men——"

"You are positive the murderer could not have slipped by you all, as the door flew open, and so made his escape?"

"That was utterly impossible. We were all grouped around the door and stayed so, until we entered the sitting room ourselves. There was nobody there but Aunt Ursula, herself——"

"Dead?"

"Yes, but only just dead. Polly heard her faint moans, after her loud screams, you know, before we broke in."

"And what were the words she used when she screamed out?"

"I don't know exactly, but they were cries for help, and I'm sure Polly said she called out 'Thieves!' Of course, she was unable to speak coherently."

"Now," began Stone, "to look at this one point. Her assailant had to get out or stay in, didn't he? You're sure he didn't get out, therefore he must have stayed in. A man of flesh and blood cannot go through walls, like a ghost."

"But he didn't stay in!" cried Iris. "We searched the room at once, there was nobody in it. You know there's almost no place to hide. We looked behind the window curtains, and all such places—and, too, we were in this room continuously, till others came, and no one could have gone through here without being seen."

"Nor could he get out of the barred windows. Then what became of him?"

"Ah, Mr. Stone," said Hughes, "that's the question that has puzzled us all. If you can solve that, we can begin to look for the murderer!"

"Meantime, we must assume him to be a spook? Is that it?" Stone smiled a little at the complacent Hughes.

"I don't say that, but I do call the manner of his exit an insoluble mystery."

"If *he* could accomplish it, *I* can find out how," Stone said, quietly. He had no air of bravado, but he made the statement in all sincerity.

"I believe you can!" declared Lucille. "That's why I wanted you, Mr. Stone. I've heard of your almost unbelievable cleverness, and I knew if anybody could get to the bottom of this mystery, you could."

"I don't mind admitting that it is seemingly the most inexplicable one I ever encountered, but I shall do my best. And I want the cooperation of you all. There are many things to be told me yet; remember I've only just heard the main details, and each of you can give me light in different ways. I'll call on you for information when necessary. Also, Miss Darrel, will you extend your hospitality to my young assistant?"

"That boy?" Lucille smiled.

"Yes; Terence, his name is. He's my right-hand man and attends to a lot of detail work for me."

"He's a handful," and Lucille laughed again. "I saw him in the kitchen, wheedling round Polly, and begging for cookies."

"I'll warrant he got 'em," said Stone. "He has a way with him that is persuasive, indeed. But he won't make you any bother. Fix him up a bed in the loft, or anywhere. He's willing to rough it."

"Oh, no, he can have a decent room, of course. I'll give him one in the garage, there's a nice one next to Campbell's."

At that moment, Terence appeared at the door.

"Come in," said Stone. "I want these ladies to know you."

Awkwardly the boy entered, and blushed furiously as Stone gravely introduced him all round.

"We'll be friends, Terence," said Iris, who felt sorry for his embarrassment, and who pleasantly offered her hand.

"Thank you, ma'am, and will you please call me Fibsy, it makes me feel more at home—like."

"Fibsy! What a funny name! Because you tell fibs?"

"Yes'm! How'd you guess?" The laughing eyes met hers and the boy's stubby paw touched Iris' soft hand.

But some subtle spark passed between them, that made each feel the other a friend, and a tacit compact was sealed without a word.

"Lemme see the room?" whispered Fibsy, with a pleading look at Fleming Stone.

"Yes," and the detective rose at once, and accompanied the lad to the room of the tragedy.

The details of the death of Mrs. Pell were quickly rehearsed, and Fibsy's eyes darted round the room, taking in every detail of walls and furniture.

Hughes was astounded. Who was this insignificant boy that he should be consulted, and referred to? Why was an experienced detective, like himself, set aside, as of no consequence, while Fleming Stone watched absorbedly the face of the urchin?

"How did the murderer get out?" Hughes could not help saying, with a view to confusing the boy.

"Gee! If all you local police has concentrated your thinkers on that all this time, and hasn't doped it out yet, I can't put it over all at once! But Mr. Stone, he'll yank the heart out o' the mystery, you can just bet. Of course, 'How'd the murderer get out?' is easy enough to sit around an' say—like a flock of parrots! The thing to do is to find out how he *did* get out!"

Fibsy stood, hands in pockets, in front of the mantel, looking down at the floor.

"Here's where she was lyin'?" he asked gravely, and Iris nodded her head.

Leaning down, Fibsy looked up the chimney, and Hughes laughed out.

"Back number!" he said, looking bored, "Don't you s'pose we've investigated that chimney business? A monkey couldn't get up that little flue, let alone an able-bodied man!"

"That's so, my bucko!" and Fibsy beamed on Hughes, without a trace of rancor at the elder man's scorn.

"Now about the evidence against Mr. Bannard," Stone said to the local detective, "do I understand it's only the newspaper and cigarette that he was supposed to have left in this room——"

"Well," Hughes defended himself, "he had motive, he was seen around these parts, and he denies he was up here——"

"Never mind, I'll talk with him, please. I'll learn more from his own story."

"He isn't guilty, oh, Mr. Stone, he *isn't* guilty!" Iris exclaimed, her beautiful eyes filling with tears. "Please get him out of that awful jail, can't you?"

"Let us hope so, Miss Clyde." Stone spoke abstractedly. "Where is the newspaper in question?"

"Here it is," and Iris took it from a drawer and handed it to him.

"Why, this has never been opened," exclaimed Stone.

"No," agreed Hughes, "when Bannard came up here Sunday morning on his bicycle, he had no thought for the day's news! He had other plans ahead. He carried that paper up here without reading it, and he left it here, also unopened."

"Might 'a' been opened an' folded up again," offered Fibsy. "It has, too."

"I did that," said Hughes, importantly. "I opened it, the first time I saw it, naturally one would, and I refolded it exactly as it was. It's of no further value as evidence, but I made sure it hadn't been read. You can always tell if a paper's been read or not."

"Sure you can," agreed Fibsy. "Where's this Mr. Bannard live?"

"In bachelor apartments in New York," said Iris.

"I mean, *where* in New York?" the boy persisted

"West Forty-fourth Street."

"He ain't the murderer," and Fibsy handed the newspaper, that he had been glancing over, back to Hughes.

"You darling!" cried Iris, excitedly, grasping Fibsy's two hands. "Of course he isn't. But how do you know?"

"Don't go too fast, Fibs," said Fleming Stone, smiling with understanding at the boy. "Shall we say the real murderer lives somewhere near Bob Grady's place?"

"Yes, sir, *yes!* O Lord, what a muddle!"

Again the boy stood in front of the fireplace, musing deeply.

"New?" he said, turning to the electric lamp on the nearby table.

"Yes," said Iris, puzzled at his actions. "When the man knocked Auntie down the table was overturned and the lamp smashed to bits. We put a new one in its place."

"Oh, all right. Now where was that cigarette stub found, and how far was it burned?"

Hughes disliked to answer the boy's questions, but Fleming Stone turned expectantly toward him, so he replied, "It was on the desk, and it was about half-smoked."

"And this poker? Did it lie here, where it is now? Wasn't she hit with it?"

"Those things have all been thrashed out," replied Hughes, a little petulantly. "No, she wasn't hit with the poker, she was flung down and her head knocked onto the sharp knob on the fender."

"How do you know?"

"There's a blood stain on the brass knob, and her head was right by it. The poker is two feet away."

"Might 'a' been used, all the same," and Fibsy stared at it. "Howsumever, that don't count. We've got her dead, and we've got to find out who did it—and, so far, it wasn't Mr. Bannard."

"When will it begin to be Mr. Bannard?" said Hughes, with fine sarcasm.

"I mean," Fibsy returned, quietly, "so far, they ain't nothin' to implicate Mr. Bannard. Somethin' might turn up, though. But I don't think so. And anyway, the problem, first of all, ain't *who*, but *how*. That's what we must hunt out first, eh, Mr. Stone?"

"Very well, Terence," Stone spoke abstractedly, "you attend to that, while I find the pin. It seems to me that is the most important thing——"

"Ain't that F. S. all over!" cried Fibsy, admiringly. "Puts his finger on the very spot! An' me a babblin' foolishness about findin' how the chappie got in!"

"You do certainly babble foolishness," flung out Hughes, unable to conceal his annoyance at the boy's forwardness, as he looked upon it.

"Yes, sir," and Fibsy's humble acceptance of Hughes' reproof had no tinge of irony. The boy was not conceited or bumptious, he was Stone's assistant, and took no orders save from his chief, but he never assumed importance on his own merit, nor behaved with insolence or impertinence to anyone. His only desire was to serve Fleming Stone, and an approving nod from the great detective was all the reward Terence Maguire desired.

And then, Fibsy seemed possessed of a new idea of some sort, for with a sudden exclamation and a word of excuse he ran from the room.

"Don't allow yourself to be annoyed by that boy, Mr. Hughes," said Stone; "he is a great help to me in any work. His manners are not intentionally rude, but sometimes he gets absorbed in an investigation, and he forgets what I've tried to teach him of courtesy and consideration for others. He's of humble birth, but I'm endeavoring to make him of gentlemanly behaviour. And I'm succeeding, on the whole, but in emergency the fervor of his soul runs away with the intent of his mind. For he wants to behave as I ask him to, I know that. Therefore, I forgive him much, and I must ask you to be also lenient."

Then, apparently feeling that he had done his duty by Hughes, the detective turned his attention to the room once more.

He scrutinized everything all over again. He left no minutest portion of the mantel, the table, the desk or the window draperies uninspected. A few taps at walls and partitions brought the comment, "No secret entrance, and had there been, you people must have found it 'ere this. It is a satisfaction to find so much of the investigating done already—and thoroughly done."

Hughes bridled with satisfaction, and eagerly watched Stone's further procedure.

Fibsy took his way to the garage, and began a desultory conversation with Campbell, the chauffeur.

"Who's the college perfessor?" he asked, pointing a thumb over his shoulder at a long, lank figure, hovering toward them.

"Him? He's Sam."

"Sam?"

"Yep."

"Don't babble on so! I don't want all his family history. Quit talking, can't you?"

As Campbell had said only a few monosyllables, and as he had the Scotchman's national sense of humor, he merely stared at his interlocutor.

"Oh, well, since you're in a chattering mood, spill a little more. Who's he, in America?"

"Sam? Oh, he's Agnes' half-brother, and he's half-witted."

"H'm. Sort of fractional currency! Is he—is he exclusive?"

"Eh?"

"Never mind, thank you. I'll be my own intelligence office. Hey, Sam, want some chewin' gum?"

The lackwit turned to the bright-faced boy who followed him, and favored him with a vacant stare.

"Gum, sonny, gum, you know. Chew-chew! Eh?"

Sam held out his hand, and Fibsy put a paper package in it.

"Wait a minute," he went on, leading Sam out of earshot of the garage. "What's that song I heard you singing a bit ago?"

"No, sir! Sam don't sing that more."

"Oh, yes, Sam does. It's a pretty song. Come now, I like your voice. Sam sings pretty—very pretty."

The wheedlesome tone and smile did the trick, and the foolish boy broke out in a low, crooning song:

"It is a sin to steal a pin,   As well as any greater thing."

"Good!" Fibsy applauded. "Where'd you learn that, Samivel?"

"Long ago, baby days."

"And why do you sing it to-day?"

A look of fear came over Sam's face, followed by a smile of cunning. He looked like a leering gargoyle, as grotesque as any on Notre Dame.

"You know why?" he whispered.

"Oh, yes, I know why. But we won't tell anybody, will us?"

"No, not anybody."

"Who'd you steal it from?"

"From chair, he, he! From old Mister Chair."

"Yes, of course," and Fibsy's heart beat fast. "The big, fat Mister Chair?"

"Yes, big fat Mister Chair!"

"In Mrs. Pell's room?"

"Yes, yes, in Missy Pell's room."

But Fibsy began to think the clouded intellect was merely repeating words spoken to it, and he asked, "Who put pin in chair for Sam to steal?"

"Who?" and the blank, foolish face was inquiring.

"Campbell?"

"No, no! not Campbell!"

"No, no, it was Agnes."

"No! not Agnes——"

"Who, then?" Fibsy held his breath, lest he disturb the evident effort the poor lad was making to remember.

"Missy Iris," Sam said at last, "yes, Missy Iris, Missy Iris—yes, Missy——"

"There, there," Fibsy shut him up, "don't say that again. Did you see her?"

"Yes, by window. Then, Sam steal pin. It is a sin to steal a pin. It is a sin to steal a pin—it is——"

But Fibsy set to work to turn the poor befuddled mind in another direction, and after a time he succeeded.

"There are two things to find," Fleming Stone said, "the murderer and the pin. There are two things to find out, how the murderer got away, and why the pin is valuable."

Stone persisted in his belief that the pin was of value, and that in some way it would lead to the discovery of the jewels. He had read all of Ursula Pell's diary, and though it gave no definite assurance, there were hints in it that strengthened his theory. Before he had been in the Pell house twenty-four hours, he had learned all he could from the examination of the whole premises and the inspection of all the papers and books in Mrs. Pell's desk. He declared that the murderer was after the pin, and that, failing to find it, he had maltreated Ursula Pell in a fit of rage at his failure.

"She was of an irritating nature, you tell me," Stone said, "and it may well be that she not only refused to give up the pin, but teased and tantalized the intruder who sought it."

"But what use *could* the pin be as a clue to the jewels?" Lucille Darrel asked. "I can't imagine any theory that would explain that."

"I can imagine a theory," Stone responded, "but it is merely a theory—a surmise, rather; and it is so doubtful, at best, I'd rather not divulge it at present. But the pin must be found."

"I haven't found it, but I've a notion of which way to look," said Fibsy, who had just entered the room.

It was Mrs. Pell's sitting room, and Fleming Stone was still fingering some packets of papers in the desk.

"Out with it, Fibs, for I'm going over to see Mr. Bannard now, and I want all your information before I go."

So Fibsy told of what Sam had said, and of the snatch of song he had sung.

"Good enough as far as it goes," commented Stone, "but your source of knowledge seems a bit uncertain."

"That's just it," said Fibsy. "That's why I didn't tell you this last night. I thought I'd tackle friend Boobikins this morning and see if I could get more of the real goods. But, nixie. Sam says he has the pin, but he doesn't know where it is."

"I'm afraid you're trying to draw water from an empty well, son; better try some other green fields and pastures new."

"I know it, Mr. Stone, but s'pose you just speak to the innocent before you go away. You can tell if he knows anything."

"Why should Sam steal the pin?" Iris asked, her eyes big with amazement.

"You can't tell *what* such people will do," Fibsy returned. "He may have seen you hiding it, as he says he did, and he may have come in and stolen it, just because of a mere whimsey in his brain. Is he around here much?"

"Quite a good deal, of late. He's fond of Agnes, and he trails her about, like a dog after its master. Aunt Ursula wouldn't have him around much when she was here, but Miss Darrel doesn't mind."

"I don't like him," said Lucille, "but I am sorry for him, and he does adore Agnes. I think he ought to be put in an institution."

"Oh, no," said Iris, "he isn't bad enough for that. He's not really insane, just feeble-minded. He's perfectly harmless."

"Bring him in here," suggested Stone.

Fibsy ran out, and came back with the half-witted boy.

"Hello, Sam," said Stone, in an off-handed, kindly way, "you're the boy for us. Now, where did you say you found that pin?"

"Here," and Sam pushed his hand down in the big chair, in the very spot where Iris had concealed it.

"Good boy! How'd you get in this room?"

"Through window in other room—walked in here!" He spoke with pride in his achievement. But at Stone's next question, a look of deep cunning came into his eyes, and he shook his head. For the detective said, "Where is the pin now, Sam?"

The lack-luster eyes gleamed with an uncanny wisdom, and the stupid face showed a stubborn denial, as he said, "I donno, I donno, I donno."

And then he broke forth again into the droning song:

"It is a sin to steal a pin,
As well as any greater thing!"

This couplet he repeated, in his peculiarly insistent way, until they were all nearly frantic.

"Stop that!" ordered Lucille. "Put him out of the room, somebody. Hush up, Sam!"

"Wait a minute," said Stone, "listen, Sam, what will you take to show me where the pin is?"

"Dollars, dollars—a lot of dollars!"

"Two?" and Stone drew out his wallet.

"Yes, 'two, three, four—lot of dollars!"

"And then you'll tell us where the pin is?"

"Yes, Sam tell then—it is a sin——"

"Don't sing that again. Look, here's four nice dollar bills; now where's the pin?"

"Where?" Sam looked utterly blank. "Where's the pin? Nice pin, oh, pinny, pin, pin! Where's the pin? Oh, *I* know!"

"All right, where?"

"Forgot! All forgot. Nice pin forgot—forgot—forgot——"

"Oh, pshaw!" exclaimed Lucille, "he doesn't know anything! I don't believe he really took the pin at all. He heard Agnes and Polly talking about it and he thinks he did."

"Oh, yes, Sam took pin!" declared the idiot boy, himself. "Yes, Sam took pin—pinny-pin—beautiful day, beautiful day, beautiful—beautiful day!"

The boy stood babbling. He was not ill-looking, and the pathos of it all made him far from ridiculous. A tall, well-formed lad, his face would have been really attractive, had the light of intelligence blessed it.

But his blue eyes were vacant, his lips were not firm, and his head turned unsteadily from side to side. Yet, now and again, a gleam of cunning showed in his expression, and Fibsy, watching such moments, tried to make him speak rationally.

"Think it up, Sam," he said, kindly. "There! You remember now! So you do! Where did you put the nice pin?"

"In the crack of the floor! In the crack of the floor! In the——"

"Yes, of course you did!" encouraged Stone. "That was a good place. Now, what floor was it? This room?"

"No, oh, nony no! Not this floor, no, no, no—'nother floor."

But all further effort to learn what floor was unsuccessful. Indeed, they didn't really think the boy had hidden the pin in a floor crack, or at least they could not feel sure of it.

"He never had the pin at all," Lucille asserted, "he heard the others talking about it, probably they said it might be in a crack, and he remembered the idea."

"Keep him on the place," Stone told them, as he prepared to go to see Bannard. "Don't let Sam get away, whatever you do."

*   *   *   *   *

The call on Winston Bannard was preceded by a short visit to Detective Hughes.

While the lesser detective was not annoyed or offended at Stone's taking up the case, yet it was part of his professional pride to be able to tell his more distinguished colleague any new points he could get hold of. And, to-day, Hughes had received back from a local handwriting expert the letter that had been sent to Iris.

"And he says," Hughes told the tale, "he says, Barlow does, that that letter is in Win Bannard's writing, but disguised!"

"What!" and Stone eyed the document incredulously.

"Yep, Barlow says so, and he's an expert, he is. See, those twirly y's and those extra long-looped g's are just like these here in a lot of letters of Bannard's."

"Are these in Bannard's writing?"

"Yes, those are all his. You can see from their contents. Now, this here note signed William Ashton has the same peculiarities."

"Yes, I see that. Do you believe Bannard wrote this letter to his cousin?"

"She ain't exactly his cousin, only a half way sort of one."

"I know; never mind that now. Do you think Bannard wrote the note?"

"Yes, I do. I believe Win Bannard is after that pin, so's he can find them jewels——"

"Oh, then you think the pin is a guide to the jewels?"

"Well, it must be, as you say so. 'Tenny rate, the murderer wanted something, awful bad. It never seemed like he was after just money, or he'd 'a' come at night, don't you think so?"

"Perhaps."

"Well, say it was Win, there's nothing to offset that theory. And everything to point toward it. Moreover, there's no other suspect."

"William Ashton? Rodney Pollock?"

"All the same man," opined Hughes, "and all—Winston Bannard!"

"Oh, I don't know——"

"How you going to get around that letter? Can't you see yourself it's Bannard's writing disguised? And not very much disguised, at that. Why, look at the capital W! The one in William and this one in his own signature are almost identical."

"Why didn't he try to disguise them?"

"He did disguise the whole letter, but he forgot now and then. They always do. It's mighty hard, Barlow says, to keep up the disguise all through. They're sure to slip up, and return to their natural formation of the letters here and there."

"I suppose that's so. Shall I confront Bannard with this?"

"If you like. You're in charge. At least, I'm in with you. I don't want to run counter to your ideas in any way."

"Thank you, Mr. Hughes. I appreciate the justice and courtesy of your attitude toward me, and I thank you for it."

"But it don't extend to that boy—that cub of yours!"

"Terence?" Fleming Stone laughed. "All right, I'll tell him to keep out of your way. He'll not bother you, Mr. Hughes."

"Thank you, sir. Shall I go over to the jail with you?"

"No, I'd rather go alone. But as to this theory of yours. You blame Bannard for all the details of this thing? Do you think he kidnapped Miss Clyde last Sunday?"

"I think it was his doing. Of course, the two people who carried her off were merely tools of the master mind. Bannard could have directed them as well as anybody else."

"He could, surely. Now, here's another thing—I want to trace the house where Miss Clyde was taken. Seems to me that would help a lot."

"Lord, man! How can you find that?"

"Do you know any nearby town where there's an insurance agent named Clement Foster?"

"Sure I do; he lives over in Meadville."

"Then Meadville is very likely the place where that house is."

"How do you know?"

"I don't *know*. But I asked Miss Clyde to think of anything in the room she was in that might be indicative, and she told of a calendar with that agent's name on it. It's only a chance, but it is likely that the calendar was in the same town that the agent lives and works in."

"Of course it is! Very likely! You *are* a smart chap, ain't you!"

Mr. Hughes' admiration was so full and frank that Stone smiled.

"That isn't a very difficult deduction," he said, "but we must verify it. This afternoon, we'll drive over there with Miss Clyde, and see if we can track down the house we're after."

*   *   *   *   *

Fleming Stone went alone to his interview with Winston Barnard. He found the young man willing to talk, but hopelessly dejected.

"There's no use, Mr. Stone," he said, after some roundabout conversation, "I'll be railroaded through. I didn't kill my aunt, but the circumstantial evidence is so desperately strong against me that nobody will believe me innocent. They can't prove it, because they can't find out how I got in, or rather out, but as there's nobody else to suspect, they'll stick to me."

"How *did* you get out?"

"Not being in, I didn't get out at all."

"I mean when you were there in the morning!"

Winston Bannard turned white and bestowed on his interlocutor a glance of utter despair.

"For Heaven's sake!" he exclaimed, "you've been in Berrien less than two days, and you've got that, have you?"

"I have, Mr. Bannard, and before we go further, let me say that I am your friend, and that I do not think you are guilty of murder or of theft."

"Thank you, Mr. Stone," and Bannard interrupted him to grasp his hand. "That's the first word of cheer I've had! My lawyer is a half-hearted champion, because he believes in his soul that I did it!"

"Have you told him the whole truth?"

"I have not! I couldn't! Every bit of it would only drag me deeper into the mire of inexplicable mystery."

"Will you tell it all to me?"

"Gladly, if you'll promise to believe me."

"I can't promise that, blindly, but I'll tell you that I think I shall be able to recognize the truth as you tell it. Did you write the letter signed William Ashton?"

"Lord, no! Why would I do that?"

"To get the pin——"

"Now, hold on, before we go further, Mr. Stone, do satisfy my curiosity. Is that pin, that foolish, common little pin of any value?"

"I think so, Mr. Bannard. I can't tell until I see it——"

"But man, why *see* it? It's just like any common pin! I examined it myself, and it isn't bent or twisted, or different in any way from millions of other pins."

"Quite evidently then, you've not tried to get possession of it. Your scorn of it is sincere, I'm certain."

"You may be! I've no interest in that pin, for I know it was only a fool joke of Aunt Ursula's to tease poor little Iris."

"Her joking habit was most annoying, was it not?"

"All of that, and then some! She was a terror! Why, I simply couldn't keep on living with her. She made my life a burden. And she did the same by Iris. What that girl has suffered! But the last straw was the worst. Why, for years and years Aunt Ursula told of the valuable diamond pin she had bequeathed to Iris; at least, we thought she said diamond pin, but she said dime an' pin, I suppose."

"Yes, I know all about that; it *was* a cruel jest, unless—as I hope—the pin is really of value. But never mind that now. Tell me your story of that fatal Sunday."

"Here goes, then. I was out with the boys the night before, and I lost a lot of money at bridge. I was hard up, and I told one of the fellows I'd come up to Berrien the next day and touch Aunt Ursula for a present. She often gave me a check, if I could catch her in the right mood. So, next day, Sunday morning, I started on my bicycle and came up here."

"What time did you leave New York?"

"'Long about nine, I guess. It was a heavenly day, and I dawdled some, for I wanted to get here after Iris had gone to church. I wanted to see Aunt Ursula alone, and then if I got the money, I wanted to go back to New York and not spend the day here."

"Pardon this question—are you in love with Miss Clyde?"

"I am, Mr. Stone, but she doesn't care for me. She thinks me a ne'er-do-well, and perhaps I am, but truly, I had turned over a new leaf and, if Iris would have smiled on me, I was going to live right ever after. But I knew she wasn't overanxious to see me, so I planned to make my call at Pellbrook and get away while she was absent at church."

"You reached the house, then, after Miss Clyde had gone?"

"Yes, and the servants had all gone; at least, I didn't see any of them. I went in at the front door, and I found Aunt Pell in her own sitting-room. She was glad to see me, she was in a very amiable mood, and when I asked her for some money, she willingly took her check-book and drew me a check for five thousand dollars. I was amazed, for I had expected to have to coax her for it."

"And then?"

"Then I stayed about half an hour, not longer, for Aunt Ursula, though kind enough, seemed absent-minded, or rather, wrapped in her own thoughts, and when I said I'd be going, she made no demur, and I went."

"At what time was this?"

"I've thought the thing over, Mr. Stone, and though I'm not positive I think I reached Pellbrook at quarter before eleven and left it about quarter after eleven."

"Leaving your aunt perfectly well and quite as usual?"

"Yes, so far as I know, save that, as I told you, she was preoccupied in her manner."

"You had a New York paper?"

"Yes, a *Herald*."

"Where did you buy it?"

"Nowhere. I have one left at my door every morning. I read it before I left my rooms, but I put part of it in my pocket, as I usually do, in case I wanted to look at it again."

"You know there was a *Herald* found in the room after the murder?"

"Of course I do, but it was not mine."

"What became of yours?"

"I haven't the least idea, I never thought of it again."

"Quite a coincidence, that a *Herald* should have been left there when your aunt took quite another New York paper!"

"I'm telling you this thing just as it happened, Mr. Stone."

Bannard spoke sternly, and with such a straightforward glance that Fleming Stone said, "I beg your pardon—proceed."

"I went down to New York," Bannard resumed, "and I stopped at the Red Fox Inn for lunch."

"At what time?"

"About noon, or a bit later. I don't know these hours exactly for I had no notion I'd be called to account for them, and I paid little heed to the time. I had the money I wanted, Aunt Ursula had given it to me willingly, I could pay off my debts, and I meant then to live a less haphazard life. I was making all sorts of plans to make good, and so gain Iris Clyde's favor, and perhaps, later, her love. I've not told her of this, for next thing I knew, I was suspected of killing my aunt!"

"But I'm told that the detectives have inquired, and the waiter who served you at the inn, says you were on your way *toward* Berrien, not *from* it."

"Then that waiter lies. I was on my way back to New York. I lunched at the inn, and proceeded on my way. I reached town about three or later, and when I finally got back to my rooms, I found a telegram from Iris to come right up here. I did so, and the rest of my story is public information. Now, the murderer, whoever he may have been, came to the house long after I left it. Oh, I can't say that, for he may have been hidden in the house when I was there. But, anyway, he killed Aunt Ursula about the middle of the afternoon, so I supposed my true story would be sufficient alibi. But it hasn't proved so, and now, if they say the Inn people declare I was coming north instead of going south, as I was, then I can only say that the villain who did the deed is trying to make it seem to have been me."

"That's my belief," agreed Stone; "the whole affair is a carefully planned and deep-laid scheme, and concocted in a clever and diabolically ingenious brain."

CHAPTER 15: IN THE COLOLE

Fibsy stuck to half-witted Sam like a leech. The boy's theory was that Sam had stolen the pin, as he said, and that he had hidden it with the cunning of a defective mind, in a place most unlikely to be suspected. So Fibsy cultivated the lackwit's acquaintance and established friendly relations.

Agnes rather resented Fibsy's attitude, but his wheedlesome ways won her heart, too, and the three were often together.

In fact, Fibsy enlisted Agnes on his side, and convinced her that they must learn from Sam where the pin was hidden, if he had really stolen it.

It was difficult to get information from Sam himself, for his statements were contradictory and misleading. But, by watching him closely, Fibsy hoped to catch him off guard, and make him reveal his secret.

Sam babbled of the pin continually. As Agnes said, whenever he got a new topic in his poor, disordered brain, he harped on it day and night.

"Pinny, pin, pin," he would chant, in his sing-song way, "nice pinny, pin, pin, where are you? Where are you? Nice pinny-pin, where are you?"

It was enough to drive one frantic, but Fibsy encouraged it as a means toward an end.

And one day he found Sam down on his knees poking a sharp-pointed stick in between the boards of the kitchen floor. The cracks were wide in the old house, and Fibsy held his breath as he, himself unseen, watched the idiot boy diligently digging.

But it amounted to nothing. After turning out many little piles of dust and dirt, Sam rose, and said, dejectedly, "No pinny-pin there! Where is it? Oh, oh, oh— *where* is it?"

Fibsy had learned the workings of the queer mind, and he was sure now that Sam had hidden the pin, but not in a floor crack. The mention of that hiding-place had been made by Sam to turn suspicion from the real one, and then the idea had stuck in his head, and, Fibsy feared, he had forgotten the true place of concealment.

This would be a catastrophe, for it might then be the pin would never be found! So Fibsy stuck to his self-imposed task of standing by Sam, hoping for a chance revelation.

"Go ahead," Fleming Stone told him, "do all you can with Sam. I, too, feel sure he took the pin from the chair, where Miss Clyde put it. Find the pin, Fibsy boy, find the pin, and I'll do the rest."

Stone spent an entire morning in Mrs. Pell's room, going over her old letters and getting every possible light on her earlier life.

He learned that she had been born and reared in a small town in Maine, that she had married and gone abroad for a stay of several years, that after that she had lived in Chicago, and for the past ten years had resided at Pellbrook. Her husband had died fifteen years ago, and left her his great fortune, mostly in precious stones. Ten years ago, when she came to Berrien, she had taken all the jewels from the bankers' and had concealed them in some place of safety which was not known to any one but herself.

Her diary attested this fact, over and over again. But it gave no hint as to where the hiding-place might be.

Stone pondered long and deeply over the statement that the gems were in some crypt, and, as he thought, a great inspiration came to him.

"Of course!" he said to himself, "it *is* that! It can be nothing else!"

But he confided his new theory to nobody; he only began to ask more questions.

He quizzed Iris as to her Chicago visit, and wanted a detailed account of every minute she had spent there. Then he asked her more particularly about the house where she was taken in the little motor car.

"Let's try to find it," Stone said, "let's go now."

They started off in a runabout, which Stone drove himself. Knowing that the house might be in Meadville, they went that way.

Iris was unable to verify the route, so they went there on the chance.

"A wild goose chase, probably," Stone conceded, "but we'll make a stab at it. You see, Miss Clyde, I'm getting the thing narrowed down to a few main propositions. There is, first, a master mind at the head of all the mystery. He is the murderer, he is your caller, Pollock, he is William Ashton, he is the man you saw in Chicago, who attacked you that night in Mrs. Pell's room, who kidnapped you that Sunday—in fact, he is the man at the helm. He has underlings, but I do not think they are accomplices or confederates, they are merely hirelings. Now, of course, Pollock is not this man's real name, but we will call him that for identification among ourselves. This Pollock wanted the pin, we'll say, and not only the pin, but the paper, the receipt that was in the Florentine pocket-book, and that was definitely bequeathed to Mr. Bannard. That paper is quite as valuable as the pin, and he did get that."

"Why, that was just a receipt——"

"Yes, and the pin was just a pin! But we want them both, and therefore we want the man, Pollock."

"This is Meadville, but I don't see any house that could possibly be the one they took me to. It had rather high stone front steps, with brick uprights to them."

They soon went through the little town, but no such peculiarity was to be found.

"Don't give up the ship too easily," said Stone, smiling at Iris' frown of disappointment, "we haven't exhausted our resources yet."

A few inquiries showed him the office of Clement Foster, the insurance agent.

Here Iris saw a calendar exactly like the one that had been in the room where Flossie searched her.

After a little talk, Fleming Stone discovered that the agent had given out few of those calendars outside his home town, but he mentioned some names that he remembered.

"Do any of these people live in a house with high stone steps?" the detective queried.

"Lemme see; yes, Joe Young, over to East Fallville, has stone steps."

"With brick uprights?" asked Iris, eagerly.

"Yes, that's right. Nice little house it is, too. Right on Maple Avenue, the prettiest street in that village."

Thanking the agent, the inquiring pair went on their way, rejoicing. And sure enough the house of Joe Young proved to be the very one where Iris had been taken.

They went in, and after introducing himself Stone learned that Mr. Young was decidedly interested in the Pellbrook mystery, and that his father had built the well-safe in Mrs. Pell's room.

Moreover, Young had attended the inquest, and had kept in touch with all the developments so far as he could learn them.

But it was impossible to associate him with the kidnapping of Iris. He was too frankly interested and sympathetic to be suspected of playing a part or deceiving them in his attitude toward them.

"Where were you a week ago Sunday?" Stone asked him suddenly.

"Why, let me think. Oh, yes, my wife and I went over to Meadville and spent the day with her mother's folks. Yes, that's what we did. Why?"

"Who was here in this house?" Stone went on.

"Nobody. It was locked up all day."

"Has anyone a key to it, excepting yourself?"

"No, nobody. Oh, yes, my brother has, but he's in Chicago."

"Was he in Chicago then?"

"Why, yes, I s'pose so. I don't know. Why?"

"Could he have come here that day, without your knowing it?"

"Of course he could have done so, and now you speak of it, I remember my wife said she smelt cigar smoke when we came home. I didn't notice it myself."

"What's your brother's name?"

"Young, Charlie Young. Is he up to anything wrong?"

"Is he apt to be?"

"Well, I wouldn't put it past him. Charlie's a case! I've tried to do well by him, but he's been a thorn in my side for years. I'm always expecting to have him turn up in trouble of one sort or another. Yes, if you ask me, he might have been here that day, and cut up any sort of monkey-shines!"

"Do you know any young lady named Flossie?"

"Nope, never heard of any, that I remember. But Charlie has queer friends, if that's what you're getting at. Say, tell me more about the Pell case, if you're from Berrien. How did the murderer get out?"

"I haven't discovered that yet, but I hope to do so. I understand your father was an expert carpenter and joiner?"

"Yes, sir, he was that. He died some four years ago, but I've many examples of his fine work. Want to see some?"

But Stone could not stay to gratify the son's pride in the paternal accomplishments and the two callers left and went back to Pellbrook.

"There's the man," said Stone, briefly. "Charlie Young is the master mind behind all this deviltry."

"Did he kill Aunt Ursula?" asked Iris with angry eyes.

"I don't say that, yet," Stone said, cautiously, "but he's the man who is after the pin and——"

The detective fell into a deep study and Iris, busy with her own thoughts, did not interrupt him.

She positively identified the house as the one to which she had been taken, and if Mr. Stone said that Charlie Young was the villain who had directed the kidnapping, though he did not appear himself, she had no doubt Stone wad right.

"And I've got a letter that Charlie Young wrote," Stone exulted. "I rather think that will go far toward freeing Mr. Bannard!"

"Oh, how?"

"I believe that Young wrote that letter signed William Ashton, and purposely made it look like the disguised hand of Winston Bannard."

"It was exactly like Win's writing, but different, too. The long-tailed letters were just like Win's."

"Yes, and that helps prove it. If Bannard had tried to disguise his own writing, the first thing he would have thought of would be *not* to make those peculiar long loops. Now their presence shows a clever trickster's effort to make the writing suggest Bannard at once, but also to suggest a disguised hand."

"That is clever! How can you ever catch such an ingenious villain? Shall you arrest him at once?"

"Oh, no, to suspect is not to accuse, until we have incontrovertible proof. But we'll get it! Lord, what a brain! And, yet, it may be easier to catch a smarty like that than a duller, more plodding mind. You see, he is so brilliant of scheme, so quick of execution, that he may well overreach himself, and tumble into a trap or two I shall set for him."

"Doubtless he knows you are here, doesn't he?"

"Surely; but that doesn't matter. If things are going as I hope, I'll bag him soon!"

"And yet you're not sure he's the murderer?"

"No, Miss Clyde, and I'm inclined to think he was not. However, we must proceed with caution, but we can work swiftly, and, I hope, reach the end soon. Matters are coming to a focus."

As they drove under the Pellbrook *porte cochere*, a strange-looking figure ran to greet them.

"Hello, darkey boy, who are *you?*" sang out Stone, as the blackamoor grinned at them.

Iris stared, and then burst out, laughing. "Why, it's Terence!" she cried. "For goodness' sake, Fibsy, what *have* you been doing?"

The boy was quite as black as any chimney sweep—indeed, as any full-blooded negro. He had run up from the cellar at the approach of the motor, and stood grinning at Iris and Stone.

"I'm on a trail," he said, "and it's a mighty dark one."

"Where will it lead you—to light?" asked Stone, smiling at the earnest, blackened face.

"I hope so, oh, Mr. Stone, I hope so! For the trail is somepin' fierce, be-lieve me!"

"Well, look out, don't get near Miss Clyde, nor me, either! You're a sight, Fibsy!"

"Yessir, I know it," and, without another word, the boy turned and disappeared down the cellar entrance.

Iris went into the house, but Stone went down to the cellar to see what Fibsy was doing. He found the boy diligently shoveling coal from one large coal bin to another. Nearby was Sam, quite as black as Fibsy, and the two were a comical sight.

Sam was seated on a box, rocking back and forth in an ecstasy of glee, and crooning, "Colole, colole, pinny-pin in colole!"

"That's what he says, Mr. Stone," Fibsy defended himself, "so if pinny-pin *is* in the coal-hole, I'm going to get her out! And if not, then Sam's fooled me again, that's all!"

"Terence Maguire! Do you mean to say you're going to hunt for a needle in a haystack—I mean a pin in a coal-hole?"

"Just that, sir. I'm onto friend Boobikins' curves, now, and I fully believe that his present dope is the answer! Anyway, I'm taking no chances."

"But, Fibs, it's impossible——"

"Sure it is, that's why I'm doing it. You run away and play, Mr. Stone, and let me work out this end. Didn't you tell me to find the pin? Well, I'm obeyin' orders."

Fibsy turned to his task again, and Stone watched him for a few minutes. The boy laboriously took up the coal in a small shovel, looked it over with sharpest scrutiny and then dumped it into the other bin.

By good luck the bins adjoined and the task was one of patience and perseverance rather than of difficulty.

Stepping toward his faithful assistant, Fleming Stone held out his hand, and said, quietly, "Put it there, Terence!"

Eagerly the little black paw slipped into the big, strong white one, and the handshake that ensued was all the reward or recognition the happy boy wanted.

Stone went upstairs again, and Fibsy whistled gaily as he continued his self-chosen task.

Sam, sitting by, cheered him on by continued assertions that he *had* thrown the pin in the coal-bin, and had *not* buried it in a crack of the floor.

And, as Fibsy had declared, he knew the half-wit now well enough to feel pretty sure when he was telling the truth and when not.

Meantime, Stone was pursuing his investigations. That afternoon he drove to Red Fox Inn. He went alone, and by dint of bribes and threats he learned that Charlie Young had been there since the day of the murder, and had instructed the waiter who had served Bannard at his Sunday luncheon to say that Bannard was coming from New York and not going to it. These instructions were made as commands and were backed up by certain forcible arguments that insured their carrying out.

It became clear, therefore, that Young was interested in making it seem that Bannard was at Pellbrook on

Sunday afternoon instead of Sunday morning, which latter Stone firmly believed to be the case.

Further discreet inquiry proved Young to be a frequent visitor at the inn, on occasions when he was in the locality, and that was said to be often, especially of late.

Stone went back, exultant, his brain working swiftly and steadily toward his solution of the many still perplexing points.

*   *   *   *   *

Later that afternoon, as it was nearing dusk, a yell from the cellar told, without words, that Fibsy's quest had succeeded.

Lucille and Iris followed Fleming Stone's flying footsteps down the stairs and found Fibsy, black but triumphant.

"Here's your pinny-pin, Mr. Stone!" he cried, exhausted from fatigue and excitement, and with perspiration streaming down his sooty face. "Don't tell me it mayn't be the one! It's gotter be—oh, F. S., it's *gotter* be!"

Only in moments of strong excitement did Terence address his employer by anything but his dignified name, but this moment was a strenuous one, and Fibsy broke loose. Tears rolled down his cheeks, as he gave the detective a pleading look.

"All right, Fibs, I've no doubt it's the one. Pins don't grow much in coal-holes, and though it may not be——" a glance at the woeful countenance made him quickly revise his speech, "But it is! I'm sure it is," he finished, smiling kindly at the big-eyed blackamoor.

"Sure! sure!" cried Sam, capering about, "nice pinny-pin! Sam put it there after Missy Iris put it in chair."

Fleming Stone looked at the pin curiously. As he had been informed, it was a common pin, of medium size, with nothing about it to distinguish it from its millions of brothers that are lost every day, everywhere.

"I'll take it up where there's a better light on it," he said, finally. "Fibsy, you're a trump, old boy, and after you've sought the assistance that a bath-tub grants, return to the sitting room, and I'll tell you of the value of your find, in words of one syllable."

Elated beyond all words, Fibsy ran away to bathe, and the others went to the sitting room that had been Ursula Pell's.

With a very strong lens, Fleming Stone examined the pin.

"This pin is worth its weight in gold, a million times over," he said, after the briefest examination. "It explains all!—your aunt's bequest, the efforts of Young to get it— but, I say, let's wait till Fibsy comes down before I tell you the pin's secret. It's his due, after he found it for us."

"Yes, indeed, wait," agreed Lucille, "he'll be down soon. I'll go and call to him to make haste."

"Don't tell me all," said Iris to Stone, as the two were left alone, "I want to wait till Terence comes—but tell me this, will it free Winston?"

"I hope so," Stone returned, "though it's another part of the mystery. But, to my mind, Mr. Bannard is freed already."

"Let me see the pin," and Iris took it in her hand. "Why, it is a common pin! How can you say there's anything peculiar about it?"

"You'll know soon," and Stone smiled at her. "Anyway, whatever else it means, it doubtless points the way to the recovery of the fortune of jewels that was bequeathed to you and Mr. Bannard."

"I don't want the fortune unless Winston is freed," said Iris, sadly; "if you think Charlie Young is the criminal, when are you going to get him? But you say you're not sure he killed Aunt Ursula."

"No, I'm not at all sure that he did," Stone returned gravely. "In fact, I'm inclined to think he did not."

"Then who did?"

But before Stone could answer, there was an agonized whelp from outside, as of an animal in pain.

"Goodness!" cried Iris, "that's Pom-pom's cry! Oh, my little dogsie! What has happened?"

She flew out of the room, and ran out on the lawn, from which direction she had heard the terrified cry.

Remembering the pin, as she ran, she stuck it carefully in her belt and hurried to the spot whence the sounds proceeded.

It was nearly dark now, and she sped across the grass, in fear for the safety of her pet.

Stone started to follow her, but Lucille appeared just then, and he paused to explain matters to her.

When they reached the lawn, Iris was nowhere to be seen, and the little dog, cruelly beaten, was whining in pain and distress.

Listening intently, Stone heard the last sounds of a disappearing motor car in the distance.

"Kidnapped again!" he cried, angrily. "And she's got the pin with her! Young, of course! Oh, how careless I've been!" and calling to Campbell, he ran toward the garage for a car.

"But how can you follow?" asked Lucille, distractedly, "you don't know which way they went, after the turn, do you?"

"No," said Stone, despairingly, "I don't."

CHAPTER 16: KIDNAPPED AGAIN

As Stone surmised, Iris was kidnapped again. When she leaned down to gather in her arms the little, yelping dog, a figure sprang from the shrubbery, and pressing a cloth into and over her mouth a man lifted her from the ground and carried her swiftly away.

Iris was a slender girl and the man had no difficulty in carrying her to a small motor car, which was waiting out in the main road. The dusk rendered them nearly invisible, and the detention of Stone by Lucille precluded what might have been a capture of the invader.

Placed in the car, Iris recognized at once that it was the same one in which she had been carried off before, and she well knew it was for the same purpose—to get possession of the pin.

But now that Stone had told her it was valuable, she had no mind to let it go easily. She sat quietly, as the car flew along, thinking hard what she would better do. She knew Stone would follow and rescue her if he had heard any signs of her departure. But the car made little noise, and the whole affair had been so quickly accomplished that Iris feared Stone knew nothing of it all. She assumed that he would naturally follow her out-of-doors, to learn what had happened to her pet dog, but he might not hasten on that errand, and a delay of a minute would make his advent of small use to her.

They had gone a mile or so, when the car turned into a little used path through the woods. Another man was driving the car, and her captor sat in the back with Iris. He still held her and kept the cloth, which smelled faintly of chloroform, over her mouth.

At last, when well into the woods, the car stopped, and the man got out, and ordered Iris to get out, too.

Her mind was made up now; she meant secretly to draw the pin from her belt, and drop it on the ground. It was running a risk of losing it, but it was a worse risk to have this man take it from her, and, too, after Fibsy's successful search of the coal bin, she felt pretty sure the boy could find the pin in the woods. She was carefully noting the trees and stones about, when the low voice of her tormentor said, "You will hand that pin over at once, if you please."

"I'll do no such thing," Iris retorted with spirit. "I am not afraid of you."

"Nor have you reason to be, if you give up the pin quietly; otherwise, you will find yourself in a sorry predicament."

"I haven't the pin with me," declared Iris, feeling the falsehood justifiable in the circumstances.

"I regret to contradict a lady, but I don't believe you."

The man was masked, but Iris recognized his voice and form and she well knew it was the man who had intruded upon her in her aunt's room that night, and she was sure it was the man who had instigated the kidnapping and search by Flossie. Moreover, she realized it was the man she had seen in Chicago.

She felt an anxiety to detain him and somehow to get him in the grip of the law, but she could think of no way to do that.

She dared not take the pin from her belt, for his eyes were upon her, and the dusk, though deepening, left sufficient light for him to observe her movements.

"Now, look here," he said, speaking more roughly, "there's no Flossie here. You don't want me to take all the pins you have in your clothing, do you?"

This suggestion, and the threatening tone of the man, frightened Iris more than all that had gone before. She was not afraid of physical violence, something in the man's manner precluded that, but she sensed his desperate determination to secure the pin, and she knew he would search her clothing for it, if she refused to hand it over.

Also, she knew there was small use in trying to fool him. Since Stone had verified the fact that there was something about that special pin that made it of value, since this man had tried devious ways to get it, and since she was absolutely at his mercy, the outlook was pretty black.

A vague hope that Fleming Stone would come to her rescue was not well founded, for how could he know that the car that carried her off had turned into that little woodland road?

She thought of appealing to the manliness or better nature of her enemy, but she knew that he would only reply that if she would give him the pin he would not trouble her further. An idea of asking help from the man who was in the driver's seat of the car brought only the same conclusion.

"Come, now," said Pollock, for it was by that name she thought of him. "I can't waste any more time. If you don't give me that pin in two seconds, I'll take it."

"Don't you dare!" exclaimed Iris, trying the effect of sheer bravado.

"Two seconds I'll give you, and they've passed. You needn't scream, for we're far from any habitation."

He came nearer to her, and touched the frill that was about the neck of her gown.

Iris was at her wits' end. She knew she would give up the pin rather than have him search her clothing for it, and yet, she meant to put off her surrender as long as possible.

His own words gave her a hint, and though knowing it could do no good, she screamed loud and long.

The sound infuriated the man, and he sprang at her, grasping her round the waist.

"Stop that!" he cried, "Stop or I'll kill you!"

His fingers were at her throat, and his frenzy was such that Iris feared he would carry out his threat on a sudden impulse.

But the strangle-hold he had on her brought his body near hers, and by chance Iris' hand was flung against his side coat pocket, where she felt what was indubitably an automatic pistol.

Pretending to faint, she let her head sink backward, and he involuntarily put his hand back of her neck to support her.

With a quick motion she snatched the pistol from his pocket without his knowledge.

Exultant, and feeling herself safe, Iris commanded him to release her.

He only laughed, and she whispered faintly, "Let me go, and I'll——"

Her voice died away as if from weakness, and he partially released his hold on her, which freed entirely her right arm.

With a wrench, she stepped back, and aiming the automatic at him, she said, quietly, "Step toward me, and I'll fire!"

With a profane exclamation, Pollock clapped his hand to his side pocket and fell back a pace or two.

"You little vixen!" he cried. "Give me that! You'll harm yourself!"

"Oh, no, I won't. But I'll harm you. Unless you give your driver orders to take me straight back home, I shall make this little weapon give good account of itself."

From where Iris now stood, she covered the two men, and her manner showed no signs of fear, as she calmly informed them that a move on the part of either would be followed by a shot.

"And," she said, "while I'm not an expert, I can manage to hit at this short range."

"Come, come, now, let's arbitrate," said Pollock, who, evidently, knew when he was cornered. "Give me the pin and I'll go halves with you."

"Halves of what?"

"Of the treasure. Oh, don't pretend you don't know all about it! Didn't that old smarty-cat you've got on the job tell you what the pin means?"

"If he did, *you* don't know," said Iris, talking blindly, for she could make no guess why the pin was a factor in the case at all.

"Don't I? I'm the only one who does know! Your Stone detective can never get a cent's worth of good out of that pin without my help. I'm the only one on earth who knows its secret, or who can turn it to use. So, now, miss, will you make terms? Wait! You needn't take my word for this. Will you agree that if you return safe home with your precious pin, and when your precious detective fails to utilize the pin's secret, you'll let me disclose it to you, and you'll give me half the value of the jewels?"

"I most certainly will not!"

"Then, listen. I swear to you that you will never find those hidden jewels. Only I can tell you what the pin means, and how it leads to your aunt's fortune. Refuse my offer, and neither you nor anyone else will ever see one tiniest gem of your aunt's hoard."

There was something in the man's voice that carried conviction. Iris was a good reader of human nature, and a surety of his truthfulness came over her.

But she was far from willing to accede to his terms.

"I do not entirely disbelieve you," she said, "but I most certainly will not give you the pin——"

"You said you didn't have it!"

"You interrupted me! I was about to say I will not give it to you, even after my return home."

"Then we'll take it now! Come on, Bob."

Evading the pointed pistol by a quick jump, Pollock dashed it from Iris' hand, having really caught her off her guard as she grew interested in their conversation. The driver, Bob, sprang toward them both, and they seized Iris between them.

A terrific scream from the girl rang through the silent woods and as the pistol struck the ground it went off with a fairly loud report.

Iris felt her senses going as the two men clutched her roughly, but managed, in spite of a restraining hand, to give another loud scream.

And it was these sounds that guided Fibsy's flying feet toward the scene of conflict.

He had come with Stone in the car that the detective had used to follow Iris from Pellbrook, but as no one knew which way to look for the kidnapper's car, they had separated, and Stone with Campbell went hunting the highroads, while Fibsy, scenting the truth, had dived into the wood.

He had heard Iris' last scream, also the noise of the automatic, and he blew a loud blast on a shrill whistle, as he hurried to the girl.

Nearing the three, Fibsy's quick eyes saw the pistol on the ground, and he snatched it up, and aimed it straight at the masked man.

"Hands up!" he cried, and Pollock turned to see a small but dauntless-looking boy threatening him.

Again endangered by his own firearm, Pollock stood at bay, raging but impotent in the face of the steady aim of the boy.

In another moment Stone came, with Campbell, in the Pell car and Iris breathed freely once more, as she felt stealthily for the pin in her belt ribbon. It was safe, and she sank down on the ground, satisfied to let the newcomers take charge of the whole matter.

This they did with neatness and dispatch.

Bidding Fibsy keep the two men covered with the small but efficacious weapon, Stone and Campbell tied the hands of Pollock and his man Bob, using the dustrobe from Pollock's car, cut into strips for the purpose.

Then they bundled them unceremoniously into their own car and Stone himself took the wheel.

Campbell drove Iris home, but Fibsy traveled with his chief.

The boy was thrilling with satisfaction at the way things were turning out, and not at all vain-glorious over his own part in the affair.

Stone turned the two men over to the police on a charge of kidnapping and then, elated, returned to Pellbrook.

"How can I be grateful enough to you," Iris cried at sight of the detective, "for coming to my aid! And Fibsy, too! Oh, what should I have done if you hadn't arrived just as you did? But how did you know where we were?"

"I didn't," said Stone; "it was Fibsy's idea that the man would take to the woods. But your screams and the noise of the revolver led us at the last. I congratulate you, Miss Clyde, on a pretty narrow escape. Those men were desperate."

"Oh, I know it! Pollock began by being fairly courteous, but when I wouldn't give up the pin, he grew rough and rude."

"Miss Clyde, we must look out for that pin. Though, now that the one who wants it is in safe-keeping himself, there's not so much danger. But he may have clever assistants. By the way, there's no doubt that this so-called Pollock is Charlie Young. Hughes is putting him through a third degree, and I think we need not concern ourselves about him just now. He won't escape from his present quarters easily."

"This child must go to bed now," said Lucille Darrel, with an affectionate glance at Iris. "She's had enough to upset any ordinary set of nerves, and she must rest."

"Yes, Miss Clyde, go now, and I think, if you leave the pin with me I'll keep it safely, and moreover, to-morrow morning, I'll tell you its secret."

"Oh, tell me now! Please do, Mr. Stone. What can it be that makes it a key to the jewels' hiding-place?"

"Not to-night. Indeed, I don't yet know its secret myself, but I hope to find it out. If I may, I'll stay alone in Mrs. Pell's sitting-room for a time, until I puzzle it out."

Iris reluctantly went off with Lucille, and the detective locked himself in the room where Mrs. Pell had met her tragic death.

He had, as his working implements, the pin, a strong magnifying glass, a thick pad of paper and a lead pencil.

As the first streaks of dawn began to show in the eastern heavens, Fleming Stone had, as results of his night's work, forty or fifty scribbled pages of the pad, all of which were in the waste basket, a small, remaining stub of lead pencil and the pin and the magnifying glass.

Also he had a heavy heart and a feeling of despair and dejection.

He went to his room for a few hours' sleep before breakfast time and when he met the family at table, he said shortly, "Finding a needle in a haystack is child's play compared to the task ahead of us."

He refused to explain until after breakfast, and then, Iris and Lucille went with him to the sitting room and the door was closed upon them. Fibsy was there, too, as the boy was never excluded from important conferences.

Stone locked the door, and then said, impressively, "The dime and pin bequeathed you by your aunt, Miss Clyde, form a far more valuable inheritance than any diamond pin I have ever seen. I congratulate you on the possession of the pin, and I ask you where the dime is."

"Gracious, I don't know," replied Iris. "I threw it out of the window the day I received it, and I've never thought of it since."

"The pin is a key to the hiding-place of the jewels, as I will explain fully in a few minutes," Stone proceeded, "but it may be necessary to recover the dime also, before we can utilize the information given us by the pin."

Iris looked bewildered, but repeated her statement as to the whereabouts of the dime.

"And again," Stone said, "the dime may be of no importance in the matter. I'm inclined to think it is not, because Pollock—or Young rather—made no effort to gain possession of the dime, did he?"

"No; I think not. That first day he called on me, as Mr. Pollock, and wanted the pin, I told him he might search the lawn for the dime if he chose, but I don't think he did so."

"I'll find the dime if it's out in the side yard," Fibsy volunteered.

"Now, I'll tell you what this pin is," resumed Stone, holding up the mysterious bit of brass. "It contains a cipher—a cryptogram."

"How can it?" asked Iris, blankly.

"On the head of this pin is engraved a series of letters which form a cipher message telling of the hiding-place of your aunt's jewels."

"On the head of that little pin! Impossible!"

"It does seem impossible, but I assure you that on the surface of the head of this pin there are thirty-nine letters, which, meaningless in themselves, form a cipher statement. If we can solve their message——"

"If we *can!*" cried Iris. "We *must!*"

"You bet Mr. Stone will work it out, if it's a cipher," Fibsy declared, looking with pride and confidence at his employer's face.

"Not so easy, Fibs," Stone returned. "It's a cryptogram which necessitates another bit of information, a keyword, before it can possibly be solved. By the way, Miss Clyde, that's what your aunt's diary means by its reference to the jewels being hidden in a crypt. If you read her diary carefully, you'll see that she very frequently abbreviates her words, not only Tues., for Tuesday, and Dec., for December, but other words, just as the whim took her. So, as we may conclude, the word crypt stands for cryptogram. And here's the cryptogram. Now, to explain this seemingly miraculous feat of engraving thirty-nine letters on the head of an ordinary pin, I'll say that it is not an unheard-of accomplishment. Several years ago, I saw on exhibition a pin with forty-five letters to it, and I have seen one or two other similar marvels. They are done, in every instance, by a most expert engraver, who has much time and infinite patience and capacity for carefulness. Indeed, it is an art all by itself, and I doubt if there are many people in the world who could accomplish it at all."

"Can you show them to me?" Iris asked, her eyes wide with wonder.

"Oh, yes, you can see them with this glass, though even with its aid you may have difficulty in making out the letters."

Iris looked long and carefully through the powerful lens, and finally declared that she could discern the letters, but could not read them clearly.

Stone passed the pin and glass to Miss Darrel, and continued, "I spent nearly the whole night over it. I have copied off the letters, so now, if the pin should be stolen, at least we have its secret. Though, I confess the secret is still a secret."

"Lemme see it," begged Fibsy, as Miss Darrel gave up the effort to make out the letters at all.

The younger eyes of the boy read them with comparative ease.

"O, I, N, V, L, D, L," he spelled out "Sounds like gibberish, but all ciphers do that—why, Mr. Stone, the letters are clear enough and you can read any cipher that ever was made up, I'll bet! You know, you first see what letter's used most, and that's E——"

"Hold on, Terence, not so fast. That's one kind of a cipher, to be sure. But this is another sort. These are the letters:

"O I N V L D L Q P S V T H P J R C R N O X X I V B A Y O D I J Y A W W K M E U

"There's no division into words, which, of course, makes it infinitely more difficult."

"Aunt Ursula was crazy over ciphers!" exclaimed Iris, "she was always making them up. But she always called them ciphers, never cryptograms, or perhaps I might have thought that crypt. was an abbreviation. But can't you guess it, Mr. Stone?"

"One doesn't guess ciphers, they must be solved. And this one is of that peculiar kind that needs an arbitrary keyword for its solution, without the knowledge of which there is little hope of ever getting the answer."

"And you give it up?"

"Oh, no, indeed? I shall solve it, but we must find the word we need to make it clear."

CHAPTER 17: THE CIPHER

"And how would the dime help, if we had it?" Iris pursued the subject.

"I'm not at all sure that it would," Stone replied, "but there must be some hint on it as to the keyword. I tried an ordinary dime, thinking the word we need might be 'Liberty' or 'United' or 'America,' But none of those would work. I tried to think out a way where the date on the dime would help——"

"But you don't know the date!"

"No; but I tried to find a way where a date would apply, but I can't think figures are needed, it's a *word* we must have."

"Words on dimes are all alike," suggested Lucille.

"Yes, but suppose a word had been engraved on this particular dime as these letters are engraved on the pin."

"Aunt Ursula would have been quite capable of such a scheme," Iris averred, "for she had most ingenious notions about puzzles and ciphers. Sometimes she would offer me a bill of large denomination, or a check for a goodly sum, if I could guess from the data she gave me what the figures were."

"And did you?"

"Never! I have no head for that sort of thing. It made my brain swim when she finally explained it to me."

"And yet I can't think the dime is necessary for the solution of this cryptogram," Stone went on, "or Young would have tried to get that also. However, now we have the man himself, he must be *made* to give up whatever knowledge he possesses."

"He won't," Iris said, positively.

Fibsy was poring over the string of letters, which he had copied from Stone's paper.

"That's so, F. S." he said, blinking thoughtfully, "there aren't enough duplicates of any letter to mean E. This is a square alphabet with a key word, sure."

"Good for you, Terence!" and Stone smiled approvingly. "You're a real genius for ciphers! Now, where's the key word to be looked for?"

"On that paper Mrs. Pell left to Mr. Bannard," and Fibsy's eyes sparkled at the idea that suddenly sprang to his brain. "Why, of course, Mr. Stone! I didn't know I was going to say that, till it just came of itself. But, don't you see? She left the pin to Miss Clyde, and the receipt to Mr. Bannard and it takes them both to solve the cipher!"

"And that receipt was stolen by the man who murdered Ursula Pell!" said Miss Darrel; "he must have known its value!"

"It may be you've had an inspiration, Fibsy," conceded Stone, "and it may be the word is not on that receipt after all. But we must use every effort to get the paper and, also, to find that dime. It may well be a word is engraved on the coin, in the same microscopic letters as these on the pinhead. We must try both means of solution. Will you hunt the dime, Fibs?"

"Sure, but I'll bet the word is on the paper. Else why'd the old lady say that Mr. Bannard would find that receipt of interest to him? And, too, as she left the jewels to two heirs, fifty-fifty, it stands to reason part of the means of finding them should be given to each party."

"That's mere conjecture," Stone said, "but we'll look up both. I've worked hours over the cipher, and I've proved to my own satisfaction that it cannot be solved without the knowledge of the one word needed. It's like the combination of a safe, you have to know the word or you can never open the door."

"Tell me a little about it, just what you mean by key word," begged Lucille, "I know nothing of ciphers."

"I make it out that this cryptogram is built on what we call the Confederacy Cipher," Stone informed her. "It is a well known plan and is much used by our own government and by others. It is the safest sort of a cipher if the key word is carefully guarded. To make it clear to you, I will put on this paper the alphabet block."

Stone took a large sheet of paper, and wrote the alphabet straight across its top. He then wrote the alphabet straight down the left hand side. He then filled in the letters in their correct rotation until he had this result

```
A B C D E F G H I J K L M N O P Q R S T U V W X Y Z
B C D E F G H I J K L M N O P Q R S T U V W X Y Z A
C D E F G H I J K L M N O P Q R S T U V W X Y Z A B
D E F G H I J K L M N O P Q R S T U V W X Y Z A B C
E F G H I J K L M N O P Q R S T U V W X Y Z A B C D
F G H I J K L M N O P Q R S T U V W X Y Z A B C D E
G H I J K L M N O P Q R S T U V W X Y Z A B C D E F
H I J K L M N O P Q R S T U V W X Y Z A B C D E F G
I J K L M N O P Q R S T U V W X Y Z A B C D E F G H
J K L M N O P Q R S T U V W X Y Z A B C D E F G H I
K L M N O P Q R S T U V W X Y Z A B C D E F G H I J
L M N O P Q R S T U V W X Y Z A B C D E F G H I J K
M N O P Q R S T U V W X Y Z A B C D E F G H I J K L
N O P Q R S T U V W X Y Z A B C D E F G H I J K L M
O P Q R S T U V W X Y Z A B C D E F G H I J K L M N
P Q R S T U V W X Y Z A B C D E F G H I J K L M N O
Q R S T U V W X Y Z A B C D E F G H I J K L M N O P
R S T U V W X Y Z A B C D E F G H I J K L M N O P Q
S T U V W X Y Z A B C D E F G H I J K L M N O P Q R
T U V W X Y Z A B C D E F G H I J K L M N O P Q R S
U V W X Y Z A B C D E F G H I J K L M N O P Q R S T
V W X Y Z A B C D E F G H I J K L M N O P Q R S T U
W X Y Z A B C D E F G H I J K L M N O P Q R S T U V
X Y Z A B C D E F G H I J K L M N O P Q R S T U V W
Y Z A B C D E F G H I J K L M N O P Q R S T U V W X
Z A B C D E F G H I J K L M N O P Q R S T U V W X Y
A B C D E F G H I J K L M N O P Q R S T U V W X Y Z
```

"The way to use this," he explained, "is to take a keyword—let us say, Darrel. Then let us suppose this message reads, 'The jewels are hidden in ——.' Of course,

I'm only supposing this to show you our difficulties. I write the message and place the code word, or keyword above it, thus:

"Dar relDar rel Darrel Da   The jewels are hidden in

"we repeat the keyword over and over as may be necessary. Then we take the first letter, D, and find it in the line across the top of our alphabet square, and the letter under D, which is T we find in the left hand perpendicular line. Now trace the D line down, and the T line across, until the two meet, which gives us W. This would be the first letter of the cipher message if the key word were Darrel, and the message like our suggested one. But the first letter of the cipher we have to solve is O, and no possible amount of guessing can go any further unless we have the key word Mrs. Pell used to guide us. See?"

"Yes, I see," and Miss Darrel nodded her head. "It's most interesting. But, as the first letter of the cipher is O, why can't you find O in your alphabet and go ahead?"

"Because there are twenty-six O's in the square, and it needs the key word to tell which of the twenty-six we want."

"It's perplexing, but I see the plan," and Lucille studied the paper, "however, I doubt if I could make it out, even if I had the word."

"Oh, yes, you could, and if we get the dime and the receipt that was in the pocket-book we can try every word on them both, and I feel sure we'll get the answer. Now, since Pollock, or Young, rather, was so desirous of getting the pin, I argue that he had the necessary key word. Therefore we must get it from him, if we can't get it ourselves, and I doubt if he'll give it up willingly."

"Of course he has the key word," Iris said, "for he told me he could find the jewels and no one else could, if I'd hand over the pin. And he offered to go halves with me! The idea!"

"And yet, if he has the key word, and won't give it up, you can never find the jewels," observed Stone.

"You don't advise me to accept his offer, do you?"

"No; Miss Clyde, I certainly do not. But there is another phase of this matter, you know. If Charlie Young stole that paper from the pocket-book he was the one who attacked your aunt——"

"And Winston Bannard is in jail in his place! Oh, Mr. Stone, let the jewels be a secondary consideration, get Win freed and Charles Young accused of the murder—he must be the guilty man!"

"It looks that way," Stone mused; "and yet, Bannard admits he was here that Sunday morning, and had an interview with his aunt. May he not have obtained possession of the receipt—oh, don't look like that! Perhaps his aunt gave it to him willingly, perhaps she told him of its value——"

"Oh, no," cried Iris, "if all that had happened, Win would have told me. No; when he discovered that the receipt was left to him and was especially referred to in the will, he was amazed and disappointed to find that old pocket-book empty."

"He seemed to be," said Stone, but his manner gave no hint of accusation of Bannard's insincerity.

"Mr. Bannard, he ain't the murderer," declared Fibsy; "and that Young, he ain't neither. Because—how'd they get out?"

"How did the murderer get out, whoever he was?" countered Stone.

"He didn't," said the boy, simply.

It was soon after that, that Hughes came to Pellbrook to report progress.

"That Charlie Young," he said, "he's a queer dick."

"Will he talk?" asked Stone.

"Talk? Nothing but! He tells the most astonishing things. He vows he's in cahoots with Winston Bannard."

"That isn't true!" Iris cried out "Win isn't guilty himself, of course, but he isn't mixed up with a man like Charlie Young, either!"

"Young says," Hughes went on, "that the note asking for the pin is in Bannard's disguised writing. He says that Bannard put him up to kidnapping Miss Clyde and getting the pin from her so they two could get the jewels and——"

"What utter rubbish!" Iris said, disdainfully. "Do you mean that Mr. Bannard wanted to get the jewels away from me? And have both his share and my own? Ridiculous!"

"It seems, Miss Clyde," Hughes stated, "that Young has part of some directions or something like that, as to where to find the jewels; and he made it up with Bannard to get the pin, which he claims is a key to their hiding-place, and the two men were to share the loot."

"I never heard such absurdity!" Iris' eyes blazed with anger. "Mr. Stone, won't you go and interview this Young, and tell him he lies?"

"I'll assuredly interview him, Miss Clyde, but suppose Mr. Bannard did have that paper—that receipt——"

"He didn't! Why, if he had, why would he confer with that bad man? Why not by means of his paper, which is, you know, lawfully his, and my pin, which was bequeathed to me, why not, those two things are all that is necessary, find the jewels by their aid?"

"That's the point," Stone said. "It does seem as if Young possesses some information of importance."

"Well," Iris went on, angrily, "now they've got the two of them there, why can't you confront Winston with Young and let them tell the truth?"

"Perhaps they won't," Hughes put in, "you know, Miss Clyde, we didn't arrest Mr. Bannard without thinking there was enough evidence against him to warrant it."

"You did! That's just what you did! There wasn't any evidence—that is, none of importance! Mr. Stone, you don't think Win guilty, do you?"

Here Iris broke down, and shaking with convulsive sobs she let Lucille lead her from the room.

"Of course she's upset," Hughes said, with sympathy in his hard voice. "But she's got trouble ahead. I think she's in love with Winston Bannard——"

"Oh, *do* you!" chirped Fibsy, unable to control his sarcasm. "Why, what perspicaciousness you have got! And you are quite right, Mr. Hughes, Miss Clyde is so much in love with that suspect of yours that she can't think straight. Now, looky here, Mr. Bannard didn't kill his aunt."

"Is that so, Bub? Well, as Mr. Dooley says, your opinion is interestin' but not convincin'."

"All right, go ahead in your own blunderin' way! But how did Mr. Bannard get out of the locked room?"

"Always fall back on that, son! It's a fine climax where you don't know what to say next! I'll answer, as I always do, how did any other murderer get out of the room?"

"He didn't," said Fibsy.

"Oho! And is he in there yet?"

"Nope. But I can't waste any more time on you, friend Hughes, I've sumphing to attend to. Mr. Stone, I'll go and get that dime now, shall I?"

"Go ahead, Fibs," Stone returned, absently, "and I'll go along with you, Hughes, and see if I can make anything out of your new prisoner."

Fibsy went first in search of Sam, and having found that defective-minded but sturdy-bodied lad, undertook to inform him as to their immediate occupation.

"See," and Fibsy showed Sam a dime, "you find me one like that in the grass, and I'll give you two of 'em!"

"Two—two for Sam!"

"Yes, three if you find one quick! Now, get busy."

Fibsy showed him how to search in the short grass of the well-kept lawn, and he himself went to work also, diligently seeking the dime Iris had flung out of the window in her irritation.

While Sam lacked intellect, he had a dogged perseverance, and he kept on grubbing about after Fibsy had become so weary and cramped that he was almost ready to postpone further search until afternoon.

They had pretty well scoured the area in which the flung coin would be likely to fall, and just as Fibsy sang out, "Give it up, Samivel, until this afternoon," the lad found it.

"Here's dime!" he cried, picking it from the grass. "Sammy find it all aloney!"

"Good for you, old chap! You're a trump! Hooray!"

"But give Sammy dimes—two—three dimes."

"You bet I will! Here—here are five dimes for Sammy!"

Eagerly the innocent received the coins, and scampered away, having no further interest in the one he had found.

Fibsy examined the dime, but could see no engraving on it, nor any letters other than those the United States Mint had put there.

The date was 1892, if that meant anything.

Carefully wrapping it in a bit of paper, Fibsy stowed it in his pocket and went into the house to await Fleming Stone's return.

And when Stone did return, it required no great discernment to see that he was dejected and discouraged.

He received the dime with a smile of hearty approval, but it was quickly followed by a reappearance of the distressed frown that betokened non-success.

"What's up, Mr. Stone?" Fibsy inquired.

"Not my luck," was the reply; "Fibs, we're up against it."

"Let her go! What's the answer?"

"Well, that Young is a hard nut to crack."

"Not for you, F. S."

"Yes, for me, or for anybody. He's got a perfect alibi."

"Always distrust the 'perfect alibi.' That's one of the first things you taught me, Mr. Stone."

"I know it, Fibs, but this alibi is unimpeachable."

"A peach of an alibi, hey?"

"That, indeed! You remember Joe Young, over at East Fallville?"

"Yes, sir, I do."

"Well, he says that his brother, Charlie Young, was at his house to dinner on that Sunday that Mrs. Pell was killed. He says Charlie arrived about half-past twelve, and he staid there until after four o'clock. Says they were together all that time. Now, that man Joe Young, is, I am sure, an honest man. Besides, his story is verified by his wife. Of course, Charlie Young declares he was at his brother's during those hours, and in the face of all the corroboration I can't disbelieve it. But, granting that alibi, who is left to suspect but Winston Bannard?"

"How'd Young catch onto all the pin and dime and receipt business, anyway?" asked Fibsy, with seeming irrelevance.

"I don't know, I'm sure."

"There's something back of that," and Fibsy wagged a sagacious nod.

"Maybe. But whatever's back of it may incriminate Young to the extent of trying to get the pin from Miss Clyde, perhaps even having stolen the receipt from Bannard, but it positively lets him out of any implication in the murder."

"Oh—I don't know."

"Why, child, if he was really at Joe Young's house from noon till four o'clock, how could he have been here at the time Mrs. Pell was killed?"

"He couldn't." Fibsy was taciturn, but his knitted brow told of deep thought.

"I got a hunch, Mr. Stone, that's all I can say for the minute—it mayn't be right, and then again it may, but—I got a hunch!"

"All right, Fibs, work it out your own way. But remember, that alibi stands. I can see a leak in a story as quickly as the next man, but that Joe Young is honest as the day, and his wife is too. And when they assert—we telephoned them, you know—when they assert that Charlie Young was there at that time, I believe he was."

"I believe it, too, Mr. Stone. Now, what about that dime?"

Fleming Stone took his strong magnifying-glass and studied the coin.

"Nothing on it, Fibs, except what belongs there. It might have been, as I hoped, that the keyword was one of these words that are stamped on, but I tried them all, any dime was all right for that. This particular ten-cent piece has no distinguishing characteristics that I can see. The date is of no help, I think, for unless I'm altogether wrong as to the type of cipher, figures are not usable. But I'll keep it safe until I'm sure it's no good."

"All right, Mr. Stone. Now, I guess I'll work on my hunch! Wanta help?"

"Yes, if it isn't beyond my power."

"Oh, come now," and Fibsy blushed scarlet at the realization that he had seemed to plume himself on his own cleverness, "but here's the way I'm goin' about it. Say I'm the murderer. Say that door's locked on this side." They were alone in Mrs. Pell's sitting room.

"Let's lock it, to help along the local color," suggested Stone, and he did so.

"Yes, sir. Now—but say, Mr. Stone, wait a minute. What became of those ropes?"

"Ropes?"

"Yes, that the murderer bound her ankles with and her wrists. Weren't we told that there were marks on her wrists and ankles where she'd been bound with ropes?"

"Yes, well, the murderer took those away with him."

"Did he 'bring 'em with him?"

"Probably."

"Then it wasn't Mr. Bannard. If he killed his aunt, which he didn't, he never came up here with a load of ropes and things! But never mind that, now. Say I'm the murderer. I've attacked the old lady and I've got the paper I wanted, and all that. Now, how do I get out!"

Fleming Stone watched the boy, fascinated. Absorbed in the spirit of his imagined predicament, Fibsy stood, his bright eyes darting about the room, as if really in search of a means of exit.

CHAPTER 18: SOLUTION AT LAST

"I am here," he muttered, "I have killed her, or, at least, she is dying—lying there on the floor, dying—I have to get out before the servants break in—I can't get out, there's no way I can get out. Mr. Stone, he *didn't* get out, because——"

"Because he wasn't in!" interrupted Fleming Stone, excitedly. "Oh, Fibs, do *you* see it that way too?"

"Sure I do! Fancy anybody untyin' a lot o' ropes, and freein' the lady and makin' a getaway, ropes and all, in two or three minutes, and besides, he *couldn't* get out!"

Fibsy stated this as triumphantly as if it were a new proposition. "The upset table," he went on, "the smashed lamp, with its long, green cord, the poor lady's dress open at the throat——"

"Yes," Stone nodded, eagerly, "yes,—and I daresay she had lace frills at her wrists and neck——"

"Of course she did! Oh, the plucky one!"

And then the two investigators put their heads together and reconstructed to their own satisfaction the whole scene of Mrs. Pell's tragic death.

"I'll go right over to see Young again," Stone said, at last, "and you skip around to see Mrs. Bowen; she'll tell you more than Miss Clyde can."

"Of course she will, and the dominie, too."

After a long argument, Fleming Stone persuaded Young that it would really be better for him to tell the truth, as to his movements on that fatal Sunday, than to persist in his falsehoods.

Stone did not tell the prisoner of his brother's confirmation of his unimpeachable alibi, but he told him that he was sure he did not murder Mrs. Pell.

"However," Stone said, "unless you tell the truth about her death, you will not only be suspected but convicted." And, finally, seeing it was his best hope, Young told his story.

"I went to the house about half-past eleven Sunday morning," he stated, "everybody had gone to church, and the old lady was there alone."

"What did you go for?"

"To get that receipt and the pin."

"Why those two things?"

"I had reason to think that they meant the discovery of her great hoard of jewels. I'm telling you all, for I want to prove that I not only did not kill the lady, but had no thought or intention of doing so."

"You took ropes along to tie her with?"

"Hardly that. I had some strong twine, as I thought she might prove fractious, and I was determined to get the pin and paper."

"How did you ever know about those things?"

"My uncle made the pin—engraved it, I mean. He was a marvelously expert engraver in the firm of Craig, Marsden & Co. After his death I came across a memorandum that gave away the secret. Not the solution of the cipher, exactly, he didn't know that himself. But a statement that he had engraved the pin for Mrs. Pell, and that, with the receipt for the work itself, it formed a direction as to where the jewels were hidden."

"And you demanded these things of her?"

"Yes, I told her the jewels belonged partly to my uncle."

"Did they?"

"No; not exactly, though Mrs. Pell had promised him some small stones, and I'm not sure she gave them to him."

"Go on, tell it all."

"I'm willing to, for my game is up, and I want to get away from a murder charge! My heavens, I'd never think of *killing* anybody!"

"Wait a minute, you say you reached the house about eleven-thirty. How did you come?"

"I was in my little car. I left that in the woodland road."

"And that's when Sam saw you."

"I suppose so. I didn't see him."

"Did you see Bannard?"

"I did. He was coming away from the house as I started toward it."

"He didn't see you?"

"No, I took good care of that."

"Then he did go away at nearly noon, and he was on his way down to New York when he stopped at the Red Fox Inn."

"Yes, his story is all true. I fixed up the Inn people to put it the other way, because I feared for my own skin."

"You *are* a fine specimen! Well, go on."

"Well, I was bound to get that pin. I asked Mrs. Pell for it, and she laughed. She wasn't a bit afraid of me. Plucky old thing! I *had* to tie her while I hunted around! She was ready to scratch my eyes out!"

"And you beat her—bruised her!"

"No more than I had to. She struggled like a wildcat."

"And you upset the table in your scrap?"

"We did not! Nor smash the lamp. Nor did I dash her to the floor. I'm telling you the exact truth, because there's so much seeming evidence against me that I'm playing safe. I searched all the room, and I found the paper, but I couldn't find the pin."

"You cut out her pocket?"

"I did, but I didn't tear open her gown at the throat, nor did I fling her to the floor to kill her on the fender. I finally untied her and went away, leaving her practically unharmed, save for a few bruises. Why, man, she was at dinner after that, with guests present."

"And where were you?"

"I went right over to my brother's—I suppose you won't believe this, you'll think he's standing by me to save my life—but it's true. I reached Joe's by half-past twelve, and I staid there till four or so. There was nobody more surprised than I to hear of Mrs. Pell's murder! I left that woman alive and well. The slight bruises were nothing, as is proved by her presence at the dinner table."

"I can't see why she didn't tell of your visit."

"She was a very peculiar woman. And she had it in for me! I think she felt that she could get me and punish me with more surety by biding her time till she could see her lawyer, or somebody like that. It seems to me in keeping with her peculiar disposition that she kept my attack on her a secret, until she chose to reveal it!"

"Mr. Young, I wouldn't believe this strange story of yours, but for your brother's statements and my absolute conviction of your brother's honesty. Both he and his wife tell a staightforward tale of your arrival and departure on that Sunday, which exactly coincides with your own. And there is other corroboration. Now, you are held here, as you know, for other reasons; kidnapping is a crime, and not a slight one, either."

"I know it, Mr. Stone, and I'll take my punishment for that, but I'm not guilty of murder. I was possessed to get hold of that pin. I planned clever schemes to get it, but they all went awry, and I became desperate. So, when I found a chance, I took it. I did Miss Clyde no real harm, and I was willing to go halves with her. The day I had two friends take her to my brother's house, he being away for the day, she was in no danger, and at but slight inconvenience. Flossie, as Miss Clyde will tell you herself, was neither rude nor ungracious."

"Never mind all that, now, give me the receipt."

Young hesitated, but a warning scowl from Stone persuaded him, and with a sigh he handed over what was without doubt the receipt in question.

"This is Winston Bannard's property," said the detective, "and you do well to give it up."

There was much to be done, but Fleming Stone was unable to resist the temptation to go home at once and work out the cryptogram, if possible, by the aid of the receipt.

The paper itself was merely a bill for the engraving on the pin. The price charged was five hundred dollars, and the bill was receipted by J. S. Ferrall, who, Young had said, was the man who did the engraving.

There were various words on the bill, both printed and written. Working with feverish intensity, Stone tried them one by one, and when he used the word Ferrall as a keyword, he found he had at last succeeded in his undertaking.

Beginning thus:

FERRALLFERRALLFERRALL
OINVLDLQPSVTHPJRCRNOX

He pursued his course by finding F in his top alphabet line. Running downward until he struck O, he noted that was in the cross line beginning with J. J, therefore was the first letter of the message. Next he found E at the top, and traced that line down to I, which gave him E for his second letter. Going on thus, he soon had the full message, which read:

"Jewels all between L and M. Seek and ye shall find."

This solved the cipher, but was far from being definite information.

In a conclave, all agreed that the message was as bewildering as the cipher itself.

Mr. Chapin could give no hint as to what was meant. Neither Iris nor Lucille Darrel could imagine what L and M stood for.

"Seems like a filing cabinet or card catalogue," suggested Stone, but Iris said her aunt had not owned such a thing.

"Well, we'll find them," Stone promised, "having this information, we'll somehow puzzle out the rest."

"Look in the dictionary or encyclopedia," put in Fibsy, who was scowling darkly in his efforts to think it out.

"You can't hide a lot of jewels in a book!" exclaimed Lucille.

"No; but there might be a paper there telling more."

However, no amount of search brought forth anything of the sort, and they all thought again.

"When were these old things hidden?" Fibsy asked suddenly.

"The receipt is dated ten years ago," said Stone, "of course that doesn't prove——"

"Where'd she live then?"

"Here," replied Iris. "But I've sometimes imagined that she took her jewels back to her old home in Maine to hide them. Hints she dropped now and then gave me that impression."

"Whereabouts in Maine?"

"In a village called Greendale."

"Her folks all live there?"

"I think her parents did——"

"What are their names? Did they begin with L or M?"

"No; both with E. They were Elmer and Emily, I think."

"Whoop! Whoop!" Fibsy sprang up in his excitement, and waved his arms triumphantly. "That's it! L and M means El and Em! Elmer and Emily!"

"Absurd!" scoffed Lucille, but Iris said, "You're right! Terence, you are right! That would be exactly like Aunt Ursula! And the jewels are buried between their two graves in the old Greendale cemetery! I dimly remember some things Auntie said, or sort of hinted at, that would just prove that very thing!"

"It sounds probable," Stone agreed, and Mr. Chapin said it was in his mind, too, that Mrs. Pell had hinted at Maine as her hoarding place, though he had partially forgotten it.

"But this is merely surmise," Stone reminded them, "and while it may be the truth, yet is it not possible that investigation will only give us further directions or more puzzles to work out?"

"It is not only possible but very probable," said Mr. Chapin. "I know my late client's character well enough to think that she made the discovery of her hoard just as difficult as she could. It was a queer twist in her brain that impelled her to play these fantastic tricks. Moreover, I can't think she would trust that fortune in gems to the lonely and unprotected earth of a cemetery."

"That's just what she would do," Iris insisted. "And really, what could be a safer hiding-place? Who would dream of digging between two old graves unless instructed to do so? And who could know of these secret and hidden instructions?"

"That's all so, Miss Clyde," Stone agreed with her. "I think it a marvellously well chosen place of concealment, and I am inclined to think the jewels themselves are there. But it may not be so. It may be we have further to look, more ciphers to solve. But, at least we are making progress. Now, who will make a trip to Maine?"

"Not I!" and Iris shook her head. "I care for the fortune, of course, but it is nothing to me beside the freedom of Mr. Bannard. I hope, Mr. Stone, that Charlie Young's confession of how he bruised and hurt poor Aunt Ursula proves Win's innocence and——"

"Not entirely, Miss Clyde. You see, we have his proof that Mr. Bannard left this house at half-past eleven, or just before Young arrived, but that won't satisfy the police that Mr. Bannard did not return at three o'clock or thereabouts."

"But he was on his way to New York then."

"So he says; but the courts insist on proof or testimony of a disinterested witness."

"But surely someone can be found who saw Win between the time he lunched at the inn, and the time he reached his rooms in New York."

"That's what we're hoping, but we haven't found that witness yet."

"Well, anyway," Iris pursued, "the people who saw him at the inn—at what time?"

"At about half-past twelve or so, I think."

"Well, their word proves that Win wasn't hidden here while we were at dinner, as some have suspected!"

"That's a good point, Miss Clyde! Now, if we can find a later witness——"

"But who did commit the murder?" asked Lucille. "You've put that Young out of the question, now, Lord knows I don't suspect Win Bannard, but who did do it?"

"And how did he get out?" added Fibsy, with the grim smile that often accompanied that unanswerable question.

"He must be found!" Iris exclaimed. "I told you at the outset, Mr. Stone, that I want to avenge Aunt Ursula's death as well as find the fortune she left."

"Even if suspicion clings to Mr. Bannard?"

"He didn't do it! All the suspicion in the world can't hurt him, because it isn't true! I shall free him, if necessary, by my own efforts! Truth must prevail. But more than that I want the murderer found. I want the mystery of his exit solved. I want to know the whole truth, and after that, we'll go to dig for the treasure. If no one knows of the meaning of the cipher message but just us few, no one else can get ahead of us, and dig before we get there. Please, please, Mr. Stone, let the jewels wait, and put all your energies toward solving the greater mystery of Aunt Ursula's death."

"A strong point in favor of Mr. Bannard," Stone said, thoughtfully, "is the fact of the clues that seemed to incriminate him. If he had been a murderer, would he have left the half-smoked cigarette, so easily traced to him? Would he have gone off with a check, drawn that very day, in his pocket?"

"And the paper! He left that!" exclaimed Lucille.

"No," said Stone, "he didn't leave that. Young left that."

"How do you know?"

"Because Young was staying at a boarding-house up in Harlem, and the New York paper, still unfolded, had in it a circular of a Harlem laundry. That's why I remarked to Terence that the man who left that came from near Bob Grady's place, which is a saloon near the laundry in question. That paper never came from the locality where Bannard lives."

"And that proved Mr. Young's presence," Fibsy said. "Just as the cigarette proved Mr. Bannard's. Now neither of those men would have left those clues if they had murdered the lady."

"I've always heard that a murderer does do just some such thoughtless thing," remarked Chapin.

"This murderer didn't," and Fibsy shook his head. "When you goin' to tell 'em, Mr. Stone?"

"Is Mrs. Bowen coming over?"

"Yes, sir, and here she comes now."

The minister's wife came hurrying into the room, and stared at the detective.

"You sent for me, Mr. Stone? I don't know anything—about——"

"Nothing that seems to you important, perhaps. But, please, answer a few simple questions. Did Mrs. Pell wear lace frills at her wrists and throat at dinner that Sunday you were here? I've asked Miss Clyde, and she can't remember."

"Yes, sir, she did. I recollect I had never seen her wearing such full and elaborate ones before."

"Did you notice anything else peculiar about her attire?"

"Only a spot of blood on the instep of her white stocking."

"Did you make any mention of it?"

"No; I thought at the time a mosquito had bitten her. But afterward I heard it remarked at the inquest that her ankles had been tied and cut by cords until they bled a little. I can't see how that could have happened before dinner."

"That's just when it did happen. I think, my friends, that I will now tell you what I am positive is the truth of this matter, though it will at first seem to you incredible. Will you let me reconstruct the whole day, as far as I can. Mrs. Pell was on her verandah, when her niece and her servants went to church. Soon after Winston Bannard came. They went into Mrs. Pell's sitting room, and she willingly gave her nephew a check for a large amount. Bannard went away, leaving behind a half-burned cigarette, but nothing else that we know of. Immediately came Charlie Young. He entered Mrs. Pell's sitting room, and found her there alone. The house doors were all open. He demanded the pin, and, he threatened her and finally he used rough treatment. He cut out her pocket in his desperate determination to secure the pin and the receipt, which later he found in the old pocket-book.

"He tied her in a chair, that he might better make undisturbed search, and finally went away, taking with him the cords with which he had bound her, the receipt and such moneys as he had found about the room, and leaving behind his New York paper. Then, left bruised and hurt, Mrs. Pell, instead of following the procedure of the usual woman, pulled herself together, and, angry and indignant, told no one of her awful experience, but attended the dinner table and entertained her guests as if nothing untoward had occurred. She did not change her gown but she added wrist frills to conceal her bruises, and she doubtless failed to notice the stain on her stocking.

"Then, after dinner, after the guests departed and Miss Clyde had gone to her own room, Mrs. Pell went into her sitting room, to rest and perhaps to plan vengeance on her assailant. But weak from shock, perhaps ill and dizzied, she stumbled over that long cord that is attached to the table lamp, upset lamp and table, and herself fell and hit her head on the fender. Doubtless she herself pulled open the neck of her gown as she gasped her last. She called out for help, and cried 'Thieves!' in a dazed remembrance of the attack that had been made on her by the thief. She locked the door, of course, when she first entered the room. I'm told that was her invariable custom of a Sunday afternoon. Then, after the poor lady screamed out with her dying breath, the servants came and were forced to break in the door to effect an entrance."

"That's it, all right, and it all checks up," said Fibsy, solemnly. "Cause why? Cause there ain't any other explanation that'll fit all the circumstances."

Nor was there. It did all check up. Further evidence was sought and found. Witnesses proved the truth of Bannard's declarations. Sam identified Young as the man he had seen prowling round in the woods that morning, and everything fitted in like the pieces of a picture puzzle.

There was no way for a murderer to escape from that locked room, because there was no murderer and had been no murder. Young's was not a murderous assault, though it was enough to earn him his well-deserved punishment, and the fact that the servants heard the crash of the overset table and lamp proved that it had not happened at the time of Young's visit.

No one had chanced to enter Mrs. Pell's sitting-room between the call of Young and the breaking in of the door, so the ransacked desk and the opened safe were not discovered.

What had been taken from the safe they never knew, for Young declared there was nothing in it, and they partially believed him.

But the jewels which were found buried between the graves of Ursula Pell's parents, Elmer and Emily Pell, were of sufficient value to make it a matter of little moment what was stolen from the safe.

And Winston Bannard was set free and came home in triumph to the smiling girl awaiting him.

Only Fleming Stone knew that Win Bannard had been so evasive and taciturn regarding himself because he feared that if he were freed Iris might be suspected.

He gave Iris the glory of bringing about his release, and though she disclaimed it, she whispered to him, "I said I would win for Win! The only thing that bothered me was that note seemingly in your writing, though disguised."

"I know," said Bannard, "and I knew somebody did that to make it seem like me, but I couldn't think who the villain could be."

"It was all a mighty close squeak," Fibsy said, thoughtfully. "I believe the keynote was struck when Sam told me he had dropped the 'pinny-pin in the colole! If he hadn't we never would have got anywhere!"

"We wouldn't have then," said Stone, generously, "if Fibsy hadn't grubbed in the 'colole' for the pinny-pin."

"And found it!" chimed in Bannard. "In recognition of which one Terence Maguire, Esquire, shall receive, shortly, one diamond pin!"

"Aw, shucks!" said Fibsy, greatly embarrassed at the praise heaped upon him; "but," he added, "I'd like it a heap!"

And he did.

THE END

Other Resurrected Press Mysteries From Carolyn Wells

Resurrected Press Mysteries From Louis Tracy

The Albert Gate Mystery
Four men murdered and a fortune in diamonds belonging to the Turkish Sultan stolen, while the Foreign Office official in charge has gone missing. Was it a common jewelry theft or was it a case of international intrigue? This is the question that barrister detective Reginald Brett must solve.

The Bartlett Mystery
When Ronald Tower is murdered on his way to a bridge game on the yacht Sans Souci it at first appears a common crime. But as Rex Carshaw finds, a tragic case of mistaken identity leads to political scandal among the rich and powerful of New York.

The Strange Case of Mortimer Fenley
When the wealthy Mortimer Fenley is struck down by a shot from an express rifle on the steps of his mansion, detectives Winter and Furneaux of Scotland Yard must find the culprit. Was it the artist who claimed he was painting a picture at the time of the shot? The disaffected younger son? Or is there another suspect?

The Stowmarket Mystery
For five generations the Fergus-Hume family has been cursed. Each of the baronets has met a violent end. When the fifth baronet is found slain by a ceremonial Japanese dagger, suspicion falls on his cousin David. It falls to barrister detective Reginald Brett to prove his innocence and find the real murder in a case that spans two continents and as many centuries.

Visit www.resurrectedpress.com

Resurrected Press Mysteries by J. S. Fletcher

The Orange-Yellow Diamond
When an elderly pawnbroker is murdered in the London parish of Paddington, a young, down on his luck writer is accused of the crime. But then it's found the pawnbroker had had in his possession an extraordinary South African diamond worth over eighty-thousand pounds —a diamond that's now missing. It falls to Melky Rubenstein to unravel the mystery and prove the young man's innocence.

The Middle Temple Murder
When an elderly man's body is found on the steps of chambers in the Midde Temple, one of the Inns of Court, it falls to newspaperman Frank Spargo and Detective-Sergeant Rathbury to solve the crime. The murdered man, for indeed it was murder, was found with no money or identification on his person except for a piece of paper with the name and address of a young barrister. Who is the victim? Why was he killed? Who is the murderer?

Scarhaven Keep
Bassett Oliver, the famed actor, has gone missing. When Oliver fails to show for a rehearsal, aspiring playwright Richard Copplestone finds himself sent to the small village of Scarhaven on the northern coast of England to track down the actors movements. What he finds is mystery. Find the answers as Copplestone unravels the mystery of Scarhaven Keep.

Visit www.resurrectedpress.com

Resurrected Press Mysteries by Fergus Hume

The Green Mummy

Professor Braddock hoped to compare the burial practices of the Egyptians with those of the ancient Peruvians with his latest acquisition, the mummy of the last Inca, Caxas. But on arrival, the packing case proved to hold not the mummy, but the body of his assistant Sidney Bolton. It falls to Archie Hope to discover the murderer if he is to marry the professors step-daughter, Lucy Kendal. Who killed Bolton and where is the mummy? Was it the sea captain Hervey? The mysterious Don Pedro? Cockatoo the Polynesian servant? The professor, himself? And what has become of the emeralds? These are the questions that Hope must answer amongst the secrets of the past in The Green Mummy.

The Mystery of a Hansom Cab

"Truth is said to be stranger than fiction, and certainly the extraordinary murder which took place in Melbourne Friday morning goes a long way towards verifying that saying." Thus opens The Mystery of a Hansom Cab, the best selling mystery of the nineteenth century. When a man is found dead in a hansom cab one of Melbourne's leading citizens is accused of the murder. He pleads his innocence, yet refuses to give an alibi. It falls to a determined lawyer and an intrepid detective to find the truth, revealing long kept secrets along the way. Fergus Hume's first and perhaps most famous mystery... The Mystery Of A Hansom Cab.

Visit www.resurrectedpress.com

Resurrected Press Mysteries from the Dr. John Thorndyke Series

Dr. John Thorndyke Lecturer on Medical Jurisprudence and Forensic Medicine. Before Bones, before CSI, before Quincy, M.E– there was Dr. John Thorndyke solving the most baffling cases of Edwardian London using the latest tools of medical science. Read about his cases in:

The Eye of Osiris
John Bellingham, noted Egyptologist has vanished not once but twice in the same day. Now Dr, Thorndyke must unravel the tangled claims on his estate, solve the riddle of the missing man and find the "Eye of Osiris".

The Mystery of 31 New Inn
When Dr. Jervis is whisked away in a coach with no windows to an unknown location to treat a man in a coma from undivulged causes it is Dr. Thorndyke who must come up with the solution.

The Red Thumb Mark
The first of Dr. Thorndyke's cases finds him trying to prove the innocence of a young man accused of being a diamond thief despite the fact that his finger print was found at the scene of the crime.

John Thorndyke's Cases
More cases of medical mysteries as told by his trusted assistant Jervis, M.D. Eight stories of crime and deduction in Edwardian London.

Visit www.resurrectedpress.com

Resurrected Press Mysteries by John R. Watson & Arthur J. Rees

The Hampstead Mystery

High Court Justice Sir Horace Fewbanks found shot dead in his Hampstead home, a butler with a criminal past, a scorned lover and a hint of scandal. These are the elements of the Hampstead Mystery that Detective Inspector Chippenfield of Scotland Yard must unravel with the assistance of the ambitious Detective Rolfe. But will he be able to sort out the tangled threads of this case and arrest the culprit before he is upstaged by the celebrated gentleman detective Crewe. Follow the details of this amazing case at it plays out across Hampstead, London and Scotland until it reaches a stunning conclusion in the courts of the Old Bailey.

The Mystery of the Downs

When Harry Marsland was caught in a sudden down pour he sought shelter at Cliff Farm. Met at the door by a young woman clearly expecting someone else he is only too glad to get inside to wait out the storm. When they hear a noise upstairs in the deserted house they investigate only to discover the body of the farm's owner, Frank Lumsden, dead of a gunshot wound. Who then, killed Lumsden, and why? Who was the woman expecting and did she have any roll in the murder? These are the questions that private detective Crewe must answer in The Mystery of the Downs.

Visit www.resurrectedpress.com

Other Resurrected Press Mysteries

Mysteries on a Train

Before the Orient Express there was:

The Rome Express by Arthur Griffiths
A man is found dead in his first class sleeping compartment on the express from Rome to Paris. Who was his murderer? The Countess? The English General? His brother the clergy man? The maid who has disappeared? Is the French justice system up to solving the crime? Read about it in The Rome Express.

The Passenger from Calais by Arthur Griffiths
Colonel Basil Annesley finds he is the only passenger on the train from Calais to Lucerne. That is until a mysterious woman shows up at the last minute to book a compartment. Who is after her? What is her secret? Is she a criminal or a victim? Read about it in The Passenger from Calais

Visit us at www.resurrectedpress.com

About Resurrected Press

A division of Intrepid Ink, LLC, Resurrected Press is dedicated to bringing high quality, vintage books back into publication. See our entire catalogue and find out more at www.ResurrectedPress.com.

About Intrepid Ink, LLC

Intrepid Ink, LLC provides full publishing services to authors of fiction and non-fiction books, eBooks and websites. From editing to formatting, from publishing to marketing, Intrepid Ink gets your creative works into the hands of the people who want to read them. Find out more at www.IntrepidInk.com.